C000263195

SMALL EXPECTATIONS

Donald S. Murray

TWO RAVENS
PRESS

Published by Two Ravens Press Ltd.
Green Willow Croft
Rhiroy, Lochbroom
Ullapool
Ross-shire IV23 2SF

www.tworavenspress.com

ISBN: 978-1-906120-50-4

British Library Cataloguing in Publication Data: a CIP record for this book can be obtained from the British Library.

Designed and typeset in Sabon by Two Ravens Press.
Cover artwork by Douglas Robertson –
www.douglasrobertson.co.uk.
Photographs of original cover artwork by Bob Aylott.

Printed in Poland on Forest Stewardship Council-accredited paper.

The publisher gratefully acknowledges subsidy from the Scottish Arts Council towards the publication of this volume.

Scottish
Arts Council

About the Author

Donald S. Murray was born in Ness on the Isle of Lewis. A writer, teacher and journalist, his poetry and prose has been shortlisted for both the Saltire Award and Callum Macdonald Memorial Award. Author of *The Guga Hunters*, his work has also appeared in a number of national anthologies and on BBC Radio 4 and Radio Scotland. He lives and works in Shetland.

For more information about the author, see
www.tworavenspress.com

CONTENTS

EQUILOGUE

SOURCES AND INSPIRATIONS

'Now I return to this young fellow. And the communication I have got to make is that he has great expectations.'

from *Great Expectations* – Charles Dickens

'I recall with a sense of injustice my own fragmented life, the choices I had to make when I didn't realise I was making them, the losses I endured before I well knew that I was enduring them, the contradictions I was involved in before I knew they existed. And I know that my own life has been a snake pit of contradictions, because of an accident of geography and a hostile history...'

Iain Crichton Smith

PRELUDE

Scenes from a Hebridean Boyhood

1

My parents fed me with so many fish that, when I was around eight, I began to grow gills. These first revealed themselves in the shape of miniature double chins forming on either side of my throat. They were the same shade of silver as much of the rest of my skin, the tiny fins that had appeared one morning to replace my hands, and the oddly shaped head with eyes peering out from the forehead that formed above my neck and shoulders. Later, I began to have trouble walking, tumbling each day under the weight of scales. Mum and Dad grew alarmed at this and decided to starve me, in an attempt to restore me to my normal size and shape. However, their diet went too far. I became a sprat, a sliver of fish, not much larger than plankton. My parents looked at me with dejection and dismay. Eventually, they decided that there was nothing for it but to use me as bait. They thrust a tiny steel hook down my throat and cast a long, nylon line far and deep into the ocean, hoping that I might bring more worthwhile spawn to shore.

2

It was when I reached the age of ten that my parents decided I was such an embarrassment to them that there was little alternative but to hide me in a peatbank. I remember watching them as they stripped away a patch of turf from the moorland, digging through heather with the sharp blade of a spade. Later, they both grinned as they cut deep into moist, dark peat, working till they laid bare the layer of rock and stone hidden by its depths. They lifted me then, lowering me into the great and empty hollow they had made. 'You'll be alright,' they kept saying as they packed me in its chill and black decay, burying me below its surface. 'You'll be alright.' I lay there till the following summer when they took me out again, drying the peat which had crusted around my flesh. After they had turned me round a few times, ensuring that every inch of my body had been burnished brown by the sun, they hoisted me on their shoulders and carried me home. It was there that they performed the final act of my existence – tossing me on the household fire.

3

I realised how much my parents cared the day they kept urging me to rest instead of helping them, sparing me from all the hard effort of trying to scratch some pathetic excuse for life from the thin soil on our croft. 'Go and lie on the beach,' they said, shaking their heads when I suggested I should join them. I was still resting there some four hours later when the tide rolled in, washing all around me a vast counterpane of kelp that wrapped around my flesh and bones, binding me to the foreshore. Later, the sea began to rumble, pounding my skull, cracking my limbs, transforming my long curly hair into fronds of dabblelock, my arms and hands into oarweed, my legs into brown stipes of cuvie. A jewel of anemone became fixed to my chest where my heart had been; bladderwrack trailed around my groin. And when all that happened, my mother and father gathered their broken son on their backs and carried me to the field that had defeated all their strength and labour, casting all that remained of my once strong and youthful body onto the field they had ploughed and dug over, preparing my corpse to fertilise their land.

4

My parents were delighted the morning I began to possess hooves. They took me down to the village blacksmith, providing me with the first gift I ever received from them: a pair of golden horseshoes. 'Run,' they told me. 'Show me how quickly you can race.' And they boasted of my speed to their neighbours, sent me on errands across the moor to warn the people who lived there of thunderstorms or strong tides that had affected our side of the island. Eventually I grew tired of this, and headed in the direction of a sea-loch a mile or two away. I concealed myself in its depths, allowing the water to roll over my mane, waves to tumble across my flanks. I hid there for years, only emerging when the local miller came to the loch-shore, asking for help to turn the mill-wheel that he owned. It might have been his loose talk that brought my parents to the loch. They called my name aloud as they stood on its banks. After a while, I decided to answer them, stirring the dust of the earth as I towered above their heads. 'How handsome you are,' they declared. 'Will you give us a ride on your back?' I did as I was told, going faster when they urged me to do so, slowing down, too, when their heels dug into my flesh. And so I went on for hours, racing across the moor like they had asked me to do in my youth, my hooves thundering, tail flashing back and forth. Eventually, I decided I had done it long enough. I turned in the direction of the loch and drowned my parents in its depths.

SMALL EXPECTATIONS

When he was raised up by his ankles, words spilled from his mouth. Spinning round, he saw the wall of dunes by the village graveyard; the meanness of his home; the doctor's twin daughters dressed in swimsuits racing across sand. And he longed to be with them, anxious to escape the leg-irons forged for his feet; to be bright with expectations, the prospect of escape, spitting out the remnants of the Gaelic that choked him, narrowing his horizons, binding his people to this place.

Songs of Exile

1
(To T & P)

Alexina used to see her sons'
tomorrows in the glass floats
waves crashed ashore
from fishing boats.

Within the tawny shade of one,
she summoned Kenneth's future,
world witnessed through a haze of glass
that brimmed with beer or rum,

Or Alasdair's existence,
clear, opaque as that transparent gaze
fixed upon her own face
while she nursed him all his days,

Or aquamarine
where the currents
Seoras set between them
could be seen

In measurements of minches crossed,
torrents of salt she'd shed
each night she sat to contemplate
the favourite son she'd lost.

2

Cousin Murdo left these shores
to get to know the ways of trees;
the high trapeze of Douglas firs,
Sequoia's dark tunnels.
And, of course, gnarled timber
of Canada's great forestry,
its shades altering in autumn,
or in winter, bared by freeze
of winds spilling from the Arctic,
snow-blizzards bursting free.

For he'd grown tired
of the tangled paths of moorland,
how his footsteps stalled and stumbled
on a sudden shift of sand;
of scanning skylines
only to gain a sense
of human insignificance,
his size and scale made slighter
by the giant scope of seas,

And instead, he longed to be
lifted,
levitated,
set loose
among red cedar, juniper, spruce,
a patch of lodgepole pine,
spinning like a gymnast, free
of the bare tracts of his homeland,
the grasp and hold of ancestry.

3

He thought much about skeletons,
admiring the symmetry of dead sheep
rotting on the island moor,

And the brittle frames of old boats too,
white bones disintegrating
among the tick of dandelion clocks blown about the shore.

He headed to the shipyard for the chance
to see steel rising within scaffolding,
diaphragm and life restored

By welding rod and rivet,
both hull and keel like breastbone
buoyant above the ocean's floor.

4

Hugh used to think he was Houdini
suspended in straitjacket dangling high above the Minch,
fingers stretching out for padlock
so he could try to free himself – inch by endless inch –

From that cold mesh that bound him,
a knotless web of love and kin
fine as nylon monofilament
his father scooped his catch within

Each night on the *Ocean Harvest,*
a Niagara of silver gleams that he
longed so much to step over
in a breathless act of escapology

By key passed in a lover's kiss,
just as Harry slipped his chains
breaking through great falls of water
to stand on dry land once again.

5

Donald Louie used to leaf through
pages of the National Geographic,
finger trailing through rain-forests of Brazil,
wading in and out of streams of New York traffic.

But he never settled anywhere until
he plumped for Patagonia,
its plateaux as empty, flat and bare
as any Lewis moor or machair,
the swift passage of his finger pausing
as he stopped to declare:
'That's it. I've finally found it.
I think I'll settle there.'

6

All that time and he could hear it beckon,
that signal crossing boundaries,
transmitted through the kirk-walls,
through psalms and prayers he reckoned

might stop its pleading coming within reach.
All that time and yet the cry still haunted,
making him clench his eyes and fingers tight,
close his mouth lest he might speak

how he was compelled to touch another's hand,
feel the strength of blood and skin,
hear a low voice in the darkness,
longings he could not tame or understand,

yet always seemed to rule him, all
that time cajoling him
to leave home, obeying the persistent
urgency of heart and body's call.

'He is to be brought up a gentleman,'
they might have said, noting his name down
on that register they stretched out within the school in town.

'He is to be brought up a gentleman,'
– and to leave the croft's confinement and explore
more exotic latitudes than both sea and moor
that seemed to stretch out endlessly from his crofthouse door.

'He is to be brought up a gentleman,'
forsake soiled dungarees and boots to go
in borrowed suit and polished shoes and show
in exams and interviews how much he's come to know
of this existence those around him chose.

'He is to be brought up a gentleman,'
– and soon there'll come a day when the tongue
he spoke in freely back when he was young
will fail him; when stammering will become
normal when he talks it; when home will turn
cold and strange towards him and going back reminds him

there's no hope of return.

Voices in the Hebrides

1 ⮕ The Ghost Inside My Throat

My voice began to fracture from the moment I learned to speak; the attempt to master two tongues splintering my larynx as it stretched to cope with the lilt and gutturals of my native language, the dry precision of the words the coloniser had brought, the wide and warring range of consonants and vowels with which each day my young mind and open mouth were filled.

Over time, that split increased, widening as the fissure sank lower and lower within my neck, rupturing veins and arteries, the sinews and muscles of my heart, sinking deeper into my chest and stomach, tearing at my loins, until I became a life divided, a spirit shred apart, a husk deprived of words.

And there was discord in that division. It unleashed the sounds that squabbled in my voice-box, let loose the jagged rhythms of my two tongues to war on the horizon, soaring towards sky as they howled and screamed and ripped themselves apart, becoming jumbled and distorted as they charged and ran amok, fleeing from the body in which they had been enclosed too long.

Some respite came when I fixed and settled on our masters' language, learning to express myself within its limitations, its narrow choice of vowels, the close confinement of its consonants, trying to ignore and forget the days when I mourned the absence of certain sounds and rhythms within my mouth, the cadences and music of another tongue, aware at all times of how it haunts me.

The ghost inside my throat.

Because I am not using them,
never spoken and not heard,
I find that I am losing them,
the most basic, simple words.

Falt was first to disappear,
the Gaelic word for 'hair',
slipped from my skull the other night
to skulk below a rug somewhere.

And *ceann* as well has headed off,
mourning the thick grey
thatch covering it in latter years,
or, perhaps, the words it used to say

Like *amhach,* the word for 'neck'
that once held the *ceann* upright.
I noticed it had disappeared
when I shaved my chin the other night,

And my chest and arms are fading
as fundamental words slip free
from memory, forgetting to name parts
that make up my anatomy

Till my future becomes clear
as mirror blurs and dulls for me.
Soon I'll be spineless as the rest,
deprived of all identity.

3 ⇒ THE TONGUE

For a long time before that day, my tongue was growing loose within my mouth. I could feel it flap as it slipped momentarily from the back of my throat, sensing it breaking away and pushing and probing against the inside of my teeth, both molars and incisors. There was one morning when I woke to find it had wriggled away from its usual position and was squeezing its way through my closed lips, a thin edge of scarlet pushing out of my mouth as if it wished to enjoy a life independent of my body. I shoved it back, making sure it was firmly in place once more.

Yet the problem became more acute that afternoon in the library. I was talking to Maurice Settler at the time, listening to his southern English voice expound his usual theories about what my fellow Gaels should do to preserve and protect the language.

'Refuse to pay the TV licence till we have a dedicated channel on Freeview…'

'Never speak English. Not even when you're talking to someone who can only speak English…'

'You sure about that?' I questioned.

'Yes. Yes,' he said with his customary certainty, his blue-eyed gaze fixed on my face. 'Of course I'm sure. It's the only thing that can be done to preserve the language. It's got no chance otherwise. Not if its guardians are weak-kneed folk like you.'

I was wondering what all this might do to our conversation, exclusively in English, when that dancing rhythm set off in my tongue. I stuttered. I stammered, trying to frame and form words as it shifted and rippled within the confines of my mouth, performing strange, frenzied movements once again.

'I don't … I don't…'

'You alright? Cat got your tongue?'

I didn't answer. It wasn't that I didn't try to do so, but when I opened my mouth, I was conscious that my tongue was now beyond my control, a long, wet, pink organ that was unable to shape any of the sounds that came from the larynx at the back of my throat. All I could do was rasp, wheeze, produce a hoarse, low rattle which Maurice in front of me was smiling at, his blue eyes twinkling with good humour at my efforts to speak.

'Donald...?'

Even my name sounded like an insult in his mouth. He, at least, could make the right range of noises to pronounce it: an ability as maddening as any of the rest he possessed – raising an eyebrow condescendingly; pursing his lips disapprovingly; throwing back the fringe of his fine fair hair with his fingers and staring at you with his piercing blue eyes.

'You sure you're alright?'

It was at that moment I should have noticed something strange had happened to his accent. His voice had become deeper. He had suddenly and inexplicably acquired the ability to roll an 'r'. The vowels in 'you' and 'sure' sounded different. Instead, though, I was only aware of my own embarrassment, how I was capable of little more than a rush of air from the part of my anatomy that had formerly contained my tongue...

❖ ❖ ❖

It is difficult to remember all the thoughts that raced round my head the next few days. I suspected that it might have been my visit to the Russian barber, Ivan Yankovlevich, that had caused my injury. A demon with the clippers, he was rumoured to have cut the tip off a student's nose and attempted to conceal it in a sandwich. The young man had to go to the Western Infirmary and ask for it to be stitched on again.

I wondered if somehow he had been the one who had unfastened my tongue, cutting it with a quick, unnoticed clip of his scissors. Perhaps it was this that had led to its failure. I tried to think back if it was from that time my control had lessened over it, when it was no longer held in check by my will.

Or perhaps it was that night I spent with Philomela MacTaggart. Her tongue fenced with mine as we lay tangled together on the sofa in her flat. A strong muscular young woman, she had pinned me down on the cushions, kissing me again and again. I felt the warmth of her breath on my cheek; her breasts soft and firm on my chest; the tangle of her dark hair on my face and in my fingers. And all the time, her mouth was pressed against mine, giving me little chance to breathe.

'Aaaagggghhhhhh...' I gasped from time to time, as her tongue flicked against my throat, gums and larynx. 'Philomela ... Give me...'

'Donald ... Donald ... Donald...'

I heard my own name echo occasionally, as if it were resounding at the back of her throat, repeated again and again.

'Philomela ... Philomela ... Philomela ... Air ... Air ... Air...' I spluttered in response.

Eventually I managed to break free, escaping just as the first shafts of morning light added a little more colour to the faded green curtains. I stepped outside the tenement flat with my tongue bruised and hurt, my mouth utterly dry of saliva. I was unable to talk properly for a few days after that. Vowels could not be formed by my lips; consonants faltered on my tongue. I shaped words soundlessly, my attempts to speak painful and sore. For a few days after that, I checked my skin for wounds and scars, the inside of my mouth to test if everything was right within.

Later I grew even more nervous. I was reading Eliot's *The Wasteland* at the time, discovering its allusions to the Greek myth of Philomela: how a princess of that name had been raped by her brother-in-law Procne, and prevented from telling the

23

deed by having her tongue cut off. It made me wonder if I had been witness to any crimes or misdemeanours recently. Could that have been the way the perpetrators had reacted – shearing away my tongue when I had been asleep? If so, I would try to imitate her, finding a way to tell people what has happened here: to 'move the very woods and rocks to pity'.

In her case, she wove a tapestry to inform the world of how her tongue had been removed. It was a task that was beyond me, my skill at sewing roughly equivalent to my present ability to speak. All I could do was watch the world and be a silent witness, trying to discover who or what was responsible for what had happened to me.

◈ ◈ ◈

It was in a café at the University that I discovered what had actually been going on.

They were all there – Maurice and a few of his friends, the ones who haunted the Celtic Department, checking up the pronunciation of odd words that no one used any more, heaving their way through the largest, heaviest dictionaries for hours on end. They questioned me and my fellow native Gaels about this obscure vocabulary and were surprised when we were unable to answer.

'What's the Gaelic for "bustle"? "Handlebar moustache"? "Mutton-chop whiskers?" ...'

I must admit I tried to avoid even looking at them. There was Prionsais Humphries, the pseudo-Gael from Dumfries; Craig Gulliver-Palfry from somewhere west of Llanfairpwllgwyngyllgogerychwyrndrobwllllantysiliogogogoch; Hank McFadzean the Third from Stornoway, Arizona. I knew them all and had suffered on a few occasions what Flann O'Brien might have described as a truly Gaelic death at their hands – one of complete and utter boredom.

24

Yet this time, there was something completely different about them. As they sipped their coffee and feasted on bacon rolls, I recognised that the sounds rising from their table had altered. Unlike the strained and faltering manner in which they usually talked, they were speaking in Gaelic with accents that were not dissimilar to my own.

'Tha fios agamsa de dh'fheumas sinn a dhèanamh. Bruidhinn Gàidhlig fad na h-ùine...'

'Gu h-àraid nuair a tha duine nach bruidhinn Gàidhlig timcheall.'

'Tha thu ceart an sin...'

It was then that I worked it out, knowing only too well why my tongue had writhed that day in Maurice's company, how he had taken control of it as we sat there and I listened to him pontificate on the subject of the Gaelic language. Perhaps there were others, too, whom the likes of these men had silenced and commandeered, other Gaels deprived of the vocabulary they had gained growing up. Angrily, I marched up to them, my mouth framed in accusation but unable to speak.

'Uhh ... Uhhh...' I panted.

Grinning, Maurice looked up at me. 'Dè tha ceàrr? An ann balbh a tha thu?'

Prionsais, Craig, Hank and Maurice began to laugh, mocking me with their mouths and fingers. I moved away from them, knowing I had no way of making my accusation, robbed of my own tongue.

Gaelic was sewn into us like grains
of oats, turnip-seed, split potatoes
ploughs folded below earth each spring.

It took root among the small talk
villagers stacked at peat-banks
or found gleaming in green fields,

Or when the sharp blade of their tongues
cut through each crop of scandals
that was the season's harvest in some homes.

Yet now croftland lies fallow.
Winds keen through rush and nettle.
Cold showers of thistledown blow

Where potatoes stalked and blossomed
and the words of English broadcast on the air
find strange, new seed-beds on our lips.

The doctor's daughters never had their fingers torn
through turning, twisting blades of oats.

Their fair-brown hair was never snagged or soiled
by seeds of grain, the dirt of a ploughed field.

Their backs were never broken
through bending, binding sheaves.

Instead their minds were sharpened
by the leaves of books

Shifting back and forth
like the rhythm of a whetting stone

Preparing them for the cut and edge of knowledge,
unlike the girls surrounding him in youth.

Their shadows following, falling round him,
permitting no departure from his home ...

Scenes from a Hebridean Romance

Part One

It was obvious for a long time that Raonaid felt drawn to me. She revealed this by a thousand small glances, lowering her eyes when she saw me on my daily patrol around the harbour, concealing her gaze behind a wave of long dark hair. Most of all she showed the sheer strength of her attraction by seeking to deny it, walking quickly past when she found me in her path. The swift swirl of her dress was enough to leave behind a trace of the faint smell of salt for which she was renowned among the good people of the small fishing port where we both belonged. It would hover in the air like mist. One deep breath and it was as if a secret signal, a quiet invitation had passed between us.

It was one I was delighted to accept as I followed her between the harbour buildings, the cluster of small shops and cafés around the quayside. She would try sometimes to slip from me; an obvious ploy in which she pretended to evade me in order to test the strength of my affection. She would then stand still for a long time, her back pressed, for instance, against the cage where the fuel tank for fishing boats was kept. Looking out to sea, her lips would move as if she were singing to the seals stretched out long and grey on nearby rocks.

'She will come here with the wind.
 She will come here with the tide ...'

Then came the day she disappeared. I watched her make her way down to the harbour once again, carrying a half-full jute sack in her hand. She shook its contents on the rocks, her eyes glinting as she turned in my direction.

'She will come here for a short time,
    when her true self she will hide...'

A moment later and her head swirled round once again,
facing the waves as she dived into the ocean's depths.

❖ ❖ ❖

Morag seemed to fade a little more every time I looked at her.
A frail, wisp-like figure, shaken by each breeze, I would watch
her closely as she too wandered round the harbour, noting her
fair hair, pale skin, the muted colours of her clothing. Even her
eyes were a pallid shade of blue, as if all life and energy had
passed from her.

She was quiet. Her breath could not be heard when her
grandfather told his stories about ghosts and spirits that had
been seen in the waters of the harbour or the hills surrounding
its bay. The girl who had disappeared while rowing across from
the other side of the inlet. The travelling woman whose shadow
still flitted in the glen where she had been killed. She would listen
to all these tales soundlessly, not even shuddering or shivering
when those who sat nearby drew breath or shook.

Morag was particularly quiet when I was anywhere within
her vision. She bowed her head, turning away as if to show
respect to the shopkeeper's son who was in her vicinity. I felt
delighted at all this, aware that her quiet, reticent nature was
desirable and necessary in someone fit to be my wife. She would
pay due attention to my concerns and demands, never indulging
in the prattle heard from the lips of so many women I had
followed round the town.

It was for this reason that I approached her, speaking to her
one day near the fuel tank where I had once seen Raonaid, its
petrol vapours swirling round my head as I spoke to Morag

for the first time.

'Will you go out with me, Morag?'

She didn't answer.

'Will you go out with me?' I repeated.

She seemed to fade then, becoming ever more faint and insubstantial as she stood in silence before me. It was as if she were no longer flesh and blood, but ethereal and wraith-like.

'Perhaps...'

It was in no way the answer I expected – no strong assertion, no acceptance or rejection, just this hushed and baffling consideration of my request.

'Think on it,' I urged her.

'I...' Her voice drifted until it ebbed away. I watched as her body did much the same, her flesh becoming spirit, her form emptying itself out into the shadows of the late afternoon...

◈ ◈ ◈

The strangest love of my life was undoubtedly Agnes. For all the drabness of her name, she brought a great deal of colour not only to my life but to that of the fishing port where we both lived. Her exuberance brought its own vibrancy to that town's grey streets, her hair dyed various shades of purple and lilac, her coat a vivid canvas for a shimmering dance of Northern lights, the purple, blue and yellow woven into its cloth. There was also the loud tinkle of her laughter, the glow of a cigarette perched on the edge of her lips.

She was such an easy woman to follow, always so striking and visible as she strolled along, that I was surprised that other men did not do likewise. It was easy to notice the dash and sparkle of her presence as she slipped along the street. You could hear her laugh too, the easy way she spoke to others.

'Fine fish you have today,' she'd declare to Calum the fishmonger. 'Pity about the high prices you force us to pay for them.'

31

'You're looking pretty today,' she'd flatter some little girl she met. 'And my, you are getting big.'

But to me she generally had little to say. A short, quizzical expression would cross her face when she noticed me following her. Then one time I overheard her talking to one of the other women near the harbour.

'Who is that man?'

I did not trouble myself to listen to the reply, certain whoever she was asking was praising me, telling of my many virtues. This was how most of the people who lived around the harbour would answer, dependent as they were on my store for their livelihood and goods.

'Rich, is he?' she said another time, and I watched her smile as the man she was speaking to clearly answered in the affirmative. 'Rich as Midas,' he might have said.

It was overhearing this conversation that prompted me to ask her out that day. Her smile disappeared for a moment when I approached her; a change that convinced me I had somehow succeeded in stirring her heart.

'Agnes…' I said, 'I have to ask you a question.'

'Yes?'

'Would you like to come out with me?'

She seemed to give my question some consideration, a little knot of thought crossing her forehead. She took out a cigarette, lighting it slowly as she pretended not to be too eager, or spoil the suspense by speaking hastily, rushing in with a reply.

'Meet me down in the harbour at eight o'clock. Near the fuel tank… I'll give you my answer there.'

I nodded, certain of her response. 'I'll do that.'

And at that hour of night, she was standing in the same place I had seen other women before, waiting for me. There was a metal sign fastened to the wire netting beside her – DANGER. NO NAKED FLAME. I smiled wryly at the warning, conscious

32

that my heart was aflame as I dreamt of having Agnes lying naked beside me, stripped of her wonderful, gaudy clothes. A special, heady perfume filled the air, rising from the rainbow of oil that men had spilled there, red, green and purple bright on the black surface. The shades of her hair and coat imitated the amazing night-time phenomenon I had often witnessed swaying and swirling across our northern skies.

'Close your eyes…' she whispered.

I must have looked a little puzzled or concerned, for she spoke once again.

'Close your eyes. I want you only to taste my kiss.'

I did as she requested, unable to see her as she moved towards me, feeling her breath upon my cheek.

'You have followed many women in these parts. I want to show you now that you have chosen the very best.'

A little jolt passed through me, conscious that she knew of the others – Morag, Raonaid, Catriona, Mairi – that I had trailed behind in the past. But her closeness reassured me. I could almost hear her heartbeat, the 'ssssssshhhhhh' that passed from her lips.

'Hush…'

The silence continued for a short while, broken only by the noise of a match bursting into light, a sudden whoosh of heat and flame…

◈ ◈ ◈

A glow rises from my body as it becomes a bright flare twisting and turning. It towers in the darkness, turning green, yellow, purple, blue… For an instant, I hear myself shout and scream, trying to defeat the pain as it overwhelms me, transforming my flesh into a multitude of shades, changing my bones into the whitest of light. I call out in agony, writhing in all the terrors that flame can inflict on human existence, the anguish of a vile

33

and ghastly death.

And then I surrender, aware that I have become the colours that were emblazoned on Agnes' dark coat as she wandered around the harbour.

I have joined the immortals.

I have become the Northern Lights.

Love Songs From the Shoreline

1ᵉ Giving Sanctuary to a Priestess

I would like to gather eider-down for thatch,
building walls with the lift and tilt of feathers
plucked from a seabird's wingspan to make sure that they
                                                                    are strong
enough to give full shelter in the worst of winter weathers.

Its rafters could be sculpted from whale-bones that will keep
squalls and rattling storms from your unprotected head
while you lose yourself in dreams, an endless swirl and sweep
that sends us out on unknown odysseys while lying still
                                                                    in bed,

And I might curl tight around you, like the whirl of shells,
protecting nerve and flesh unsettled by the swell
of nightmare, sharing one and another's closeness when
                                                                    winds rear
and bear down hard on us, enraptured you are there.

She made of love a dogfish dinner
and tried to heat the cockles of his heart
by placing winkles, limpets down before him,
a way of making certain no riptide tugged apart
their lives with hold as strong as barnacles.

It's a grip he sometimes dislikes, wishing to be free
to step upon salt pastures, roam a patch of sand
where he could stay stranded, no longer drenched by sea
which she's washed up all around him,
dividing him from others,
with deep, unfathomable jealousies.

But within himself, he's sure this will not happen,
for if the day came round when he might start
to step outside her boundaries ,
she'd plunge a razor-shell down deep,
skewering his heart.

3 ⊨ KIN
FOR EILEEN AND ANGUS

What I most recall of summer
are your fingers digging dams,
channelling water across sand
until that stream is slammed
shut by grey slab of stone
wedged there by your hands,

And after that, the haste
to tighten that slim hold
with sand stirred quickly into paste
to try to halt the cold
stream as it races
down to where dark breakers roll

To smash and sweep away
the shallow reservoir
your small feet have paddled in;
a demolition that restores
the shoreline your hands altered
to all it was before.

Scenes of Hebridean Haunting

Part One

It is my job to help ferry them over. Even people like the ones who are around me now. The grieving and the calm. The upset and the angry. Those who are reconciled to what has happened and those who are shocked and devastated by an unexpected event. Sometimes they are laughing and smiling, joking to keep their knowledge of all that has occurred at bay. On other occasions, they are dark and silent, as if any word they dared to speak might provoke an endless gale of tears.

And on the car-deck below, there is, perhaps, the reason for their distress: the last physical remnants of the lives they have loved and lost. An elderly man or woman in a polished box. A youth perhaps, in his prime. Most distressing of all, a child in a white coffin. These remnants provide the last evidence of the deceased, the final moments when their breath shuddered to an end, leaving those who are now bereft to cry and mourn. Their grief spills over to wash against all who come into contact with them, even those of us among the crew who walk among these seats and tables, serving them their dinners or a drink to help steady heart and nerve, preparing them for the ordeal ahead. All this I have seen so many times during the years I have worked on this ship. It is, after all, part of the regular job a ferryman like me is required to do.

Yet this occasion feels different, even down to the way I came to work this morning. I am not wearing my usual uniform, the dark trousers and white shirt with its black clip-on badge carrying the ship's name, M.V. LOCHCHARON. Instead, I am wearing my jeans and checked shirt and blue jacket, the same clothes I put on the morning we drove down the A9 from

Inverness for a few days holiday in Edinburgh. My wife Andrea had sat beside me on that journey, our two kids Sharon and Jordan in the back. I even remember how my young son was talking while he sat there, pointing out the road-signs that we passed.

'Kincraig … Kincraig … Kincraig…'

'Lynchat … Lynchat … Lynchat…'

'Kingussie … Kingussie … Kingussie… That's a funny name.'

'I thought our next king was going to be called Charles,' Sharon, being her usual smart self, declared.

Andrea laughed. 'It probably is. If he doesn't do something absolutely stupid.'

I looked over, noting how happy she looked when she was away from the island, her fair hair waving in the breeze from the open car window. 'Perhaps he might change his name to Gussie. If you wrote in and suggested it.'

'Who knows? I might.'

'After all, you always get your own way.'

'Look who's talking…'

For all that I was unhappy with how slowly we were progressing, I grinned in her direction. She looked more content than I had seen her in ages, not complaining this time about her life on the island, the place I had taken her when we married. Concentrating once again on the road, my eyes fixed on the white caravan in front of us. It had slowed us down for miles and I was more than a little anxious to overtake. Its presence seemed all the more obstinate and annoying because I had the suspicion that the road narrowed just a little bit ahead, trapping us in its wake for some distance to come. Finally, I decided I had been in that position long enough, that this was the moment to put my foot down.

'I could help you write that letter, Mam,' Jordan was saying.

'You could…'

I had nearly passed the caravan when the truck loomed in front of me. I saw it coming in slow motion. Its number-plate. The bonnet with the legend SPEEDNORTH HAULAGE printed in large white letters on the green bonnet. The anguished face of its driver. I could also hear my children screaming, Andrea shouting 'Colin! Don't!' and then me swerving, the wheel between my fingers, hammering the sole of my boot on the brake...

From this moment onwards, my memory grows thin and hazy. I can only recall driving my Toyota along the harbour front of the mainland town the ferry leaves from to go to the island. Its white houses pass in a blur, barely visible in the thickness of the mist shrouding the waterfront. For once, I keep on going along the main road, not stopping to collect tickets at the terminal. Instead, I drive my car down through the mouth of the ship, just about the only vehicle to be seen within the darkness of its car-deck. A crewman wearing the usual luminous white jacket and safety helmet guides me into position, parking my car behind a hearse. He puts up his thumb when he decides I am safely in place.

'Okay...' he mouths.

Trying to make out his face, I nod back. He is not someone I recognise from my years working with the company. This might be because his features are in shadow, hidden by his headgear. He rushes away, as if he has a job to do elsewhere on board. I watch him stand with a group of men at the other end of the car-deck, their faces indistinct in the distance.

Matters became even more confusing after that. When I finally reached the passenger deck, it was emptier than I had ever seen before, even in the bleakest, harshest months of winter. Once or twice a crewman passed, or a girl who worked in the cafeteria, but there was no one I recognised. Despite this, I tried to speak to them, asking about the forecast, how many

41

passengers on board, any question I could think of to make conversation. They all raced past, rarely even acknowledging me with a nod or grin.

And then there were the passengers. They were the saddest and most unusual I had ever seen in my years working on the ferry. Among them, a grey-haired old man sat on his own in a corner of the lounge, his fingers, like his breath, shaking and trembling. A tiny edge of striped pyjamas poked out from beneath the sleeves of his tweed jacket, flapping around his thin wrists. Words dribbled from his lips, staining his unshaven chin.

'I want to be buried at home...' he declared. 'On the machair where my people are. I want to buried there. You hear me? You hear me?'

'Of course,' I said. 'I'm sure your family will do that...'

But he didn't seem to understand me. Instead, he kept repeating what he'd said before, describing, too, the sands which the graveyard looked down upon, a place where he had played as a child.

'That's where I want to go when I'm dead. You hear me? No other place. That's where I want to go. Among my own people...'

The TV was on in another corner. A white-haired presenter was quizzing a short blonde woman about the difficulties of dealing with grief and loss.

'The worst stage is normally the first stage, isn't it?' he was saying.

'Not always. Sometimes it's a little while later that it hits people...'

The only person who seemed to be watching was a young woman rocking back and forth in one of the seats, her long hair waving in a tide of black. Her eyes looked watery too, smeared black with mascara. She was clutching the fabric of her jeans, her knuckles white and tense. She looked as if she was holding something in her fingers, an object that threatened to slip from her grip.

'I didn't mean to take all these pills. I promise I didn't...'

Her words were interrupted by the arrival of another group of people in the lounge. They were led by an old woman and her husband who looked calm and peaceful as they arrived. Settling down in their seats, they gathered their few belongings around them – a small suitcase, a shopping bag or two from NEXT and MONSOON. The man patted his wife's wrinkled hand.

'We're finally underway, then...'

'Yes. Not before time.'

The quietness of their talk was interrupted by a shout from the other side of the lounge. A middle-aged man with sallow, wrinkled skin was rushing around the room, bumping into everyone he encountered. He wore a pair of filthy grey trousers, a dirt-stained coat that wrapped and flapped around him.

'One more drink ... That's all I need ... Just one more drink ... Will someone buy me one more drink?'

Among the uproar he was causing, it was difficult to hear the television. A newscaster was on, the antithesis of the man who was doing all the shouting. His dark hair was combed to perfection, blue tie fastened firmly in place, as he talked about a crash that had occurred on what he called 'one of Scotland's worst accident blackspots' – the A9 just outside Kingussie.

'It is believed that the occupants of the car, four members of one family, were killed in the crash. Police are withholding their names till next-of-kin are informed...'

It was then I saw Andrea enter the lounge, our two children by her side. Her eyes were tight and narrow in accusation...

Haunted by Frank Ifield

For years the elder never danced
till that Friday night in Rodel
when a long-forgotten yodel
(*I Remember You*) seeped from the hotel walls
and in that moment he recalled
romancing with this Lewis girl
he'd whirled round the Village Hall.

That memory a pinnacle
of life among these Harris hills
emerging from the distant past
till he became aware he still
dreamed of spinning in that waltz,
or stepping beside her lightning feet
when she danced the Quadrille.

And so he dreamed about her
as he jigged and reeled among a field of ewes,
remembering how she'd asked him
to attend a dance in Gravir,
and how legs had swirled below him
and he'd asked to be excused.
An hour he now regretted –
that instant he refused.
Especially now he'd come to hate
this life he did not choose.

Haunted by Elvis Presley

Daft as one,
he'd lift a brush
while sweeping out the roadside verge,
making out he held a guitar

Or strumming on his spade
while swivelling hips,
pretending he was Elvis,
a faded, greying star,

Till he perished like him too,
dining on convenience foods,
his stomach rock'n'rolling
with the swell

Of one who lived on Lonely Street,
unable even to meet the cost
of hiring out some floorspace
at the old Heartbreak Hotel.

Haunted by Dusty Springfield

She saw the father through the son,
hearing inflections of the young man's voice
in the way an old man read his sermons,
finding lessons in both prayer and psalm,
the Second Book of Samuel.
(O Absalom, Absalom, wherefore art thou, Absalom?)

Traces, too, of the strength of fingers
lifting up and taking on
the weight of that black Book;
the sweet intensity of the look
he swept over congregations
stirring in his offspring's eyes
evenings she slipped through the church-pews
with eyes lashed with mascara, blonde beehive,

Where she sat and thought that she could tame him
and reach the void his father
could not contact when he preached,
only to discover lessons
time and tears can sometimes teach –
that when you seek to fence free spirits,
the mesh of flesh and heart
required for love can topple
as it grows both frail and weak.

Scenes from a Hebridean Romance

Part Two

Valentine's Day in the Hebrides

Not knowing the correct address of the man she spent her nights and days longing for, Xanthia MacCrimmon sent Valentine cards that year to every John Macleod who lived on the island. Hordes of lipstick-covered envelopes weighed down the local post-vans as scores of quilted hearts, cute bunnies and SWALKs were delivered to households throughout the community, from north to south, east to west, country to town. The local postmen looked wearily at each items in their bag, the continual injunctions they received:

'Postie! Postie! Don't be slow!
Be like Elvis. Go, man, go…'

And then there were the looks they were given on doorsteps. Some sons appeared disappointed to see their father's name on the envelope; others were surprised. Their daughters were incredulous that the old men who humphed and coughed and scratched their crotches every evening could ever inspire such passion, especially from an unknown source.

There were also the men themselves. They took the envelope from the postman's hands in a variety of ways. Some gave an embarrassed laugh, as if to declare:

'It's been a long time since I got one of those.'

Others shoved their cards in the pockets of their overalls and dungarees, believing it might be from the women with whom they once had an affair in Adelaide, New Zealand, Sydney,

Australia or downtown Panama City. They took them to read in barns and out-buildings, trying to make out the identity of the 'X' who signed the card. For some John Macleods, this was an easy matter. There was the John who remembered the nights he had spent with a fair-haired Greek girl called Xanthia MacCrimmon; another who recalled a couple of nights in Majorca he had spent entwined in the arms of a Spanish barman called Xavier Mackenzie, a short time of passion before he returned to his life of celibacy on the croft. Others were more puzzled. Did the 'X' stand for the great kiss of betrayal they had given former lovers when they left their sides for the last time, promising they would return a short time later? Or was it a reminder of the games of noughts and crosses one John Macleod had played with his ex-girlfriend in their own strange and original version of strip poker, the loser having to remove an item of clothing? They trembled with guilt at the false promises given at that time and how they had broken them all.

Of course, there were the women too, the wives and lovers who stayed at home that day to greet the postman's arrival, believing that there might be a card or small gift on the way. Instead, they saw the envelope with their husband's name and address printed on its front, a little verse scrawled across its back:

'Violets are blue.
Roses are red.
I'm no good at poems,
But fantastic in bed...'

Some laughed at the thought of their husbands attracting any kind of romantic attention. It would have been difficult enough to envisage even some twenty years before, when they were in their physical prime. Rather than 'fantastic in bed', all they could recall was some frantic groping in the back of either Bedford vans or the delivery lorries of the carpet-fitting or building firms the men were employed by in their youth. It took a major act of imagination for them to picture their loved ones as figures that inspired female fantasy, sparking lust and love. Such stirring had not been generated by their presence years ago. It seemed even less likely now.

Others, however, had no such reassurance. They could recall an earlier incarnation of the John Macleod with whom they shared their bed and breakfast table these days. They recalled the sexual appetite their partner had displayed in the early years of their lives together, the close, almost fevered attention they had been given in the beginning of their relationship. Uneasily, they sniffed the envelopes that had arrived in their homes for clues about the kind of person who was pursuing their man. Some imagined a distinct whiff of various perfumes – Obsession? Seduction? Euphoria? Chanel No 5? – rising from the card. (One who suspected her husband of having more interest in his own gender than hers felt sure there was more than a splash of Paco Rabanne permeating that day's mail.) These women took to watching their husbands with greater suspicion than they had done hitherto. Raising binoculars in their hands, they followed their husbands' movements down the croft, wondering if it was just sickly ewes they were visiting or if some other females were enjoying the benefits of their tender ministrations. They called them up on their mobiles every time they drove to town, pretending to add one more item to the long list of shopping they had already been given.

'Just wondering if you could get some Fairy Liquid … Weetabix … A half-dozen eggs …'

In the case of one or two couples, more bad feeling was generated. There was a woman in Cairnbost who, a couple of years before, had caught her husband in the arms of a recent incomer to the village. On the evening of February 14th, she had confronted him with the card and its accusing 'X' when he came home from work. As he stammered a series of denials she refused to listen, accusing him of beginning yet another affair with some other woman who had arrived in the village.

'I saw the way you looked at her the other day in the post office,' she declared.

An hour or so later and the majority of his clothes were flapping around the garden, some of his shirts and underpants blown the length of the village in a Force 10 gale. He turned up at his sister Euphemia's door with a few remaining pairs of trousers clasped under his arm. Fierce in his innocence, he swore – both to her and anyone else who would listen – that he had no idea who might have been the 'X' who signed the card. It might even have been signed by his wife's own hand in an attempt both to get rid of him and her hands on the family croft.

Yet if at her home in Socrates Drive, Thessalonika, Xanthia MacCrimmon would have been distressed to discover this particular consequence of her actions, there was one result that would have compensated for it, appealing to the romantic within her. For years, one John Macleod had travelled to his local Free Kirk not only to worship, but also to catch sight of a sweet, shy single woman by the name of Eugenia Charleston Macleod who sat near him in the pews. Too tongue-tied to speak, he had been content for years with watching her: the quiet grace with which she slipped into her place in church; her blue tweed coat and black hat; the bun into which her fair hair had been swept and fastened onto the back of her head.

At first, he had been puzzled. On the morning the postman had given him the card, he stared at it for a long time, wondering if Eugenia had been the one responsible for its arrival. Discreet, reticent and private, the 'X' seemed to be from her. The verse, however, seemed unusual and out of keeping with her personality.

'Violets are blue.
Roses are red.
I'm no good at poems,
But fantastic in bed…'

He scratched his head for a long time before deciding there was always something about a woman that was unusual and unpredictable. He recalled that in his own mother, with her swirl of moods and tempers. Perhaps Eugenia was like that too – her blue tweed coat concealing a fierceness and passion she managed to control most of the time.

Finally, he convinced himself of this, gaining courage from a particularly learned exposition the minister made one Sunday evening from Paul's Second Letter to the Thessalonians, Chapter 3, verse 11. *('For we hear that there are some which walk among you disorderly, working not at all, but are busybodies.')* The preacher's words rang in his head as he approached Eugenia while she stood in the kirk doorway. He stuttered his suggestion that they go out together for dinner at the Fisherman's Mission.

'Will you say y-y-yes to me…?'

With her customary discretion, she whispered her acceptance of his offer. As he walked away, he knew he was the happiest John Macleod of all the John Macleods on the island, in fact of all the John Macleods on the planet, including the miserable John Macleods who lived in exile in Inverness, Aberdeen, Glasgow and the sad and distant suburbs of Lerwick. If it hadn't been a Sabbath evening, this John Macleod would have permitted himself a skip and a dance as he made his way to his orange Volkswagen Polo parked a short distance away from the kirk.

It was years later, just after their third child Rodina had been born, that John Macleod finally admitted to his wife he had been prompted to ask her out by the Valentine card she had sent. Eugenia looked at him mysteriously, wondering if he was confused in some way. Shyly, she confessed she had sent no such card, announcing that her own father, John Macleod, a seventy-odd widower, had also received a Valentine that particular February 14th. At the time, the family suspected the hand of Murdina Magdalene Campbell, a gloomy looking widow from the parish.

He shook his head in disagreement, coming to the conclusion that it was Henrietta Havisham MacHattie who had sent out an avalanche of cards that day. A stout, grey-haired woman who wore a bridal dress for years after her fiancé had jilted her on the day of their proposed wedding, she had long tormented him with coquettish winks and smiles from her position in the pews.

She was the only one desperate enough to do something like that. In an act of revenge, they decided to send her a Valentine card identical to the one he had received, an 'X' signed below a few lines of verse…

Women of the village – *What are you doing*
with your young head bowed down over the lines of a book
when there are fields to be ploughed and seeds that need sowing,
rare sunlight outside if you just care to look?

Women of the village – *Why are you reading*
while all our young daughters stand tall in the sun?
Will you raise up your head when your hairline's receding,
when your fair skin is crinkled and no longer young?

Women of the village – *When are you planning*
to set these pages aside from your unsullied hands?
There's a pattern to seasons that need man's understanding
if he's to master the ways of the land.

Scenes from a Hebridean Dining Table

Part One

Porridge Galore

(The opening scenes of this story consist of various shots of the sea breaking against a sandy coastline, men gathering on the main street of an island town, children scurrying from the doorway of an old blackhouse, the mending of nets, women spinning, the drawing down of a household blind. A commentary begins.)

Until the years of war, the people of the island of Raws were both happy and contented, enjoying the few and simple pleasures to be found in their lives.

They had all they needed – the delights of songs and stories, the warmth and glow of burning peat, a glass or two of whisky, the company of those who lived in their own home and other houses nearby.

But then in 1943, disaster overwhelmed that little community. Not famine nor pestilence, not Hitler's bombs nor the hordes of an invading army.

But something far, far worse.

The morning came when they ran totally out of porridge.

As the local bard Archie MacGillivray declared in the Post Office that day, such an occasion was a 'terrible, terrible tragedy'. It was the food the islanders most depended on, the very stuff and essence of their existence. Life without it was barely worth living. His wife Malcolmina could list all the ways it was essential to them, how they cut it into thick slices and placed into every drawer that was lying empty in their homes. They would put it into their child Matilda's schoolbag before she set off for school. It formed the basis of their soups, stews, breakfasts, dinners and desserts. It was – as the bard announced that morning – his Ambrosia, his Muse, Parnassus, food and fuel for gods and common people alike.

It was left to more practical people, such as his sister Annabellina, to explain the reasons why, for the first time in centuries, oats had failed them. Surrounded by her six children, she would try to tell them there was no porridge available, that the crops had let them down.

'It's the weather.' She shook her head sadly. 'It's been terrible, terrible, terrible lately. Every day and night, the same black wind. It turns the stalks rotten, casts away the seed into the ground. It destroys everything in its wake.'

And then Iagan Alasdair, their oldest child, would whimper, the wail of his breath like the clamour of the wind gusting outside, hacking at all that remained of their crops. His tears were like the salt borne upon its back, thrashing against all that they had planted, making sure that there would be no porridge to fill the drawers of their household for this coming season either...

◈ ◈ ◈

It was on a night like this that the *M.V. Chamberlain* went down on the rocks near the isle of Raws. The ship's captain, Mackenzie, had been down in the galley when this incident occurred, the pleasures of a good bowl of porridge obliterating all sense of what was going on around him. Its warmth forming an impregnable wall behind his ribs, he did not hear the cries of alarm from a crewman near the bow of the ship nor sense that they were sailing too close to land. And when it occurred to him that something was amiss in the moment that he rushed up in his cabin slippers to the bridge, all he did was issue a confusion of orders, his view of the sea confined by a wall of dark water, white foam smearing the glass before him.

'Starboard! Starboard!' he cried out one moment.

'Port! Port!' he called the next.

'Hell! Hell! Hell!' he bawled an instant later.

The vessel was stuck within the dreaded Maws of Raws, a set of rocks so deadly that, for generations, sailors had spoken of the treachery of that particular stretch of Lewisian gneiss. Its teeth had opened up a huge hole in the side of the vessel, one that allowed the good people of the island to go out and discover what was contained in its hold the following morning. They rowed out there as soon as they could, steering their boat through that stretch of water with all the care and knowledge only they possessed.

'Careful … Careful … Careful … 'N aire … 'N aire … 'N aire …' they declared.

And then they were out there, clambering up the rope ladder which the evacuated crew had left so conveniently over the vessel's side. They made their way across the deck and down into its hold. And then they peered into the darkness and were astonished.

Reading the words on the boxes stacked down below, their eyes gaped as widely as those of elderly American women who see Highlanders tossing the caber for the first time, gazes swirling as freely as the swing and billow of the kilt.

'Scott's Traditional …'

'Scott's Old Fashioned …'

'Quaker's …'

'The Magic Porridge Pot …'

'Reddy Brek …'

One can only imagine how the inhabitants of Raws reacted to this. It is reported that it prompted Alasdair Ann MacAndrew to perform his first handstand ever at the age of 65; that his wife Alasdairina uttered her first ever word of English – 'Superb!' – upon hearing of the discovery. (One of her children, Murchadh Beag, was reported to be so stunned by the sound from her lips that he was unable to speak at all for the following fortnight.) It is even said that the Reverend MacCodrum, the local Free Church minister, permitted himself a small smile for the first time in years at the prospect of seeing his favourite cereal before him on the kitchen table. He had long grown tired of the babbling voices of its replacement, Rice Krispies, interrupting him when he sat there, writing up the notes for his Sunday sermon.

Only one man was displeased, a retired bank manager called Captain Waggett who had come to the island from Walmington-on-Sea. Dressed in his Home Guard uniform he would march across the machair, pontificating against the backwardness of the community to which he now belonged. His dark moustache bristling, he would remonstrate with Annabel Murdag's husband, Ruaraidh Mor, about the number of children he had fathered. ('Have you never heard of continence, man?' he would declare.) He would tell Archie MacGillvray that he over-rated the importance of porridge in his life. ('There are other things, man. There are other things…') He would even lecture poor befuddled Alasadairina about the fact that she would be better off speaking English. ('You ought to try it, woman. It's the true mark of a civilised person…') And so a result of all this, they hid their discovery from Wagget's eye, dividing up the inheritance the sea had given them among the various households of the island. If he ever found them…

'We're doomed! Ah tell ye! Doomed!' Archie MacGillvray predicted.

The MacGillivrays, for instance, were granted Scott's Traditional Porridge Oats. They kept packets of it in all sorts of places, storing them in old wellington boots they warmed by their fireside. The quiet and religiously minded MacPherson family had a preference for the Quaker variety, keeping it in a hay-loft in their barn. Among others, the Macdonalds, MacCodrums, MacDougalls, MacFarquhars obtained the Reddy Brek and the Scotts Old Fashioned. Alasdairina obtained some of the latter too, but also all six packets of a brand new product, the Magic Porridge Pot. Unable to follow the English instructions on the box, she stored them away for the meantime, hiding them in the foot of the wardrobe.

And so the greatest ever era of porridge-making in the history of Raws began. In an age of rationing, people often enjoyed it three or four times a day, trying out the different tastes and textures of each brand to add a little variety to their existence. They would relish the way it slipped down their throats, the sense of warmth and fullness of their stomachs.

'There's nothing like it ... Nothing better,' Shonnie MacDougall would announce each time another helping arrived on the kitchen table. 'I can't understand men like Wagget who don't like the stuff. If you ask me, there's a big problem with them.'

The others nodded their heads. 'There's no doubt about it. The man's a couple of spoonfuls short of a full bowl.'

It was at this time that Alasdairina decided to take one of the Magic Porridge Pots out from its hiding place. One of her children, Lachina, read out the instructions to her, the little girl's voice slow and steady as she struggled to translate all that was written on the packet's side.

'Tha e gradh ...To use this pot ... airson cleachdadh a phoit ... all a person has to do is to pronounce the following spell. "Flippety, Floppety, fart, start Magic Porridge Pot, start..." If you do this, you will obtain an in-ex-haust-ib-le supply of porridge ...'

'Cha bhi thu cur cail na bhroinn?'

'No, Mum. Cha bhi. You don't put anything in it. When you want it to stop cooking, you say the words "Plippety, ploppety, plop, stop Magic Porridge Pot, stop…"'

'Well, well, well… Uil, uil, uil…' Alaisdairina announced, automatically switching into Gaelic after the hard labour of listening to English. 'Tha sinn mirbhaileach.'

And so they tried to do exactly as they were told, Alasdairina practising the instructions time and time again.

'Flippety, floppety, fart, start, Magic Porridge Pot, start…'

The pot would begin to bubble on the stove.

'Plippety, ploppety, plop, stop Magic Porridge Pot, stop…'

The bubbling of the pot would just as magically come to an end.

It wasn't long before the tale of Alasdairina's Magic Porridge Pot was told all over the Hebrides. People from all the other islands would row their boats across the Kyles of Raws, passing both the Maws and the Skerry Dubh to see its wonders. The men from Todday voyaged to the harbour in Raws, trying to forget all about the terrible shortage of whisky on their island as they tasted the magic porridge. The inhabitants of the isle of Sanday even managed to forsake their Sabbath observance for one Sunday of the year to travel south and see the miracle in their midst.

'It's like when that fellow Moses,' one of their number proclaimed, 'struck a stone with his staff to produce a flood of water. Or when they discovered manna in the desert. It's as miraculous as that.'

In the midst of it all, there was Alasdairina. She looked as content as she had ever been in her life, doling out porridge to all her visitors and pronouncing the magic words.

'Flippety, floppety, fart, start, Magic Porridge Pot, start…'

It was inevitable that Captain Wagget would eventually come to hear of it. He marched across the machair the moment the tale came to his ears, his upper lip hardening and stiffening at the thought of this modern innovation being used in a place as backward and Gaelic speaking as Alasdairina's tiny kitchen.

'It's stolen ... Stolen ... Stolen ...' he kept muttering. 'It will have to be returned right away.'

When he arrived at her home, there were even longer words. He pointed in the direction of the pot bubbling on the stove, pinning the mistress of the house in the other corner of the kitchen with a stern Napoleonic eye. Clutching her apron, she could only look terrified as he overwhelmed her with a spate of long and complex English words. Each one baffled her, leaving her confused and gasping for air.

'Do you realise, woman, that you're guilty of industrial espionage every time you use that product? Clearly it's a great commercial secret, one that they're in the process of developing for the market. And here you are using it in this backwater, this grubby little kitchen. Do you realise what might happen to you if you were ever discovered, ever found out?'

'No, Captain Wagget ... Yes, Captain Wagget...' Alasdairina mumbled.

'Do you realise you might go to prison for this terrible crime of yours? Are you aware of that?'

'No, Captain Wagget... Yes, Captain Wagget...'

While the questioning continued, so did the porridge pot. Within a short time, its contents were bubbling over its sides, foaming across the surface of the stove and onto the kitchen floor as if it were a plush, grey carpet covering every inch of the lino, coating every corner of the room. Even Captain Wagget became aware of it. He heard its rumble below the loudness of his own voice, saw it spit and bubble as it flowed in his direction, increasing in height and depth as it did so.

'Stop it, woman! Stop it!'

Alasdairina tried to do so, attempting to summon up the

magic set of words that would stop the pot from boiling and making yet more porridge. 'Pippety, poppety, pop...' she kept saying, forgetting the English words that would bring the process to an end. In her confusion, she tried instead the Gaelic ones.

'Stad! Stad! ... Sguir! Sguir!'

It was all to no avail. The porridge kept coming. It was cloaking the fireside chairs now, making its way out of her open door, covering all things with its thick and sticky warmth. In the midst of all, Captain Wagget was gesticulating, waving his arms around his head as if – for the first time in his life – he was performing a Highland fling.

'Don't panic! Don't panic!' he kept shouting as he tried to stay afloat, but neither pot nor inhabitant seemed to listen to his words. Instead, he could only watch the entire island sink in this wonderfully tasty morass, one that would cloak and conceal the entire stretch of the Hebrides and bring another vessel – this time carrying whisky to America – to crash upon the rocks near its shores...

Songs of an Inner Émigré

1

For years John sat in a Hillman Avenger
abandoned on the edge of a field of potatoes,
pressing pedals, raring to go
down the Interstate Highway to a Colorado rodeo,
Elvis' last show in Las Vegas,
his own (extremely) private Idaho,

And he didn't seem to notice
these wheels could not roll
all the way to Memphis or Chicago
even when flowers began to grow
upon the dashboard,
or blackbirds started to sing
from perches in its front wing
and a family of field-mice occupied
holes in a headlight.

Instead, he continued
to believe he could
become a star in Hollywood,
appear in Times Square New Year's Eve,
until the door disintegrated,
rust and decay
stripping away all his dreams
of downtown Dallas and LA,
finding out he could not go too far
when he looked round one day to see his vehicle
was no longer quite a car.

2

He sought to travel eastwards,
to make his way across a sea-green dial
where radio-waves tumbled,
dwindled, sprawled

in a storm of static,
till he wound up on that shore
where the voice of Radio Moscow
spread and scattered

seed to its population,
telling how the country's harvests never failed,
each year increasing yields
of wheat, potatoes, mutton,

and he thought of his poor crops,
their growth blighted by salt,
and wondered whether,
if he planted seeds behind that wall,

the surge and blast of spume might stop.

3

And, too, there was that whoosh which drew
John nightly to the chimney,
a place where even his mother knew
he dreamed continuously of seas

That might take him from this spit and slip of land –
freedom coming when winds blew
and gusted him, like paper dropped from hand
on flame, transporting him straight through

The fireplace, riding smoke and soot to places
alien to islanders – except those fabled few who knew
Babylon and Nineveh, wild Arabian spaces,
the grim backstreets of Lhasa, suburbs of Xanadu.

A TRIP TO THE MAINLAND

Dolina used to pray her guardian angels
would keep her soul secure and safe from danger
each time she stepped upon the ferry
and when she squeezed tight against a stranger's
shoulder on the bus at Ullapool,

Or when its tyres would swerve full-speed
past Corrieshalloch Gorge, Altguish and Garve,
the many swirls and curves of road
through Maryburgh and Contin,
across the Kessock Bridge and then on

To the infamy and iniquity of downtown Inverness,
where each hour she'd need shielding from
all Debenham's temptations, Boots and M&S,
the devils that assailed her, laying waste
to both her common sense and purse.

Cairstìona Beag from Cairnbost
he does not want,
for fear of inheriting her father,
an idle man who'd rather
quarrel with his neighbours
than attend to all the labours
stacked upon his croft.

Màiri Mhòr from Marnwick
he never would desire,
knowing of the perfume
of cattle, barn and byre
that often wafts around her.
He finds it's from a distance
that she is best admired.

And Doileag Dhonn from Ronasay
he prefers to stay away,
for he has come to learn
her voice is like a flight of terns
screeching as they seek to keep at bay
intruders' steps approaching
the clutch of eggs they've laid.

But the doctor's youngest girl
he would have by his side,
content within the warm caress
of champagne, foreign holidays,
                        American Express
while he whirls her round in waltzes,
whispers in her curls
what her voice had come to mean for him

The clink of far-off worlds.

Scenes from a Hebridean Dining Table

Part Two

Rhubarb

Beneath skies stacked high with rain about to fall,
between moorland's mists and Minch's squalls,
on a harsh and stony promontory,
rhubarb grows by tumbling blackhouse walls,

Long planted there by those who tried to keep
their kin at home with small bribes of a sweet
to add some savour to the cups of souse
and plates of fish each day they had to eat.

Yet it could not hold them. Man needs jam today,
tonight, tomorrow. Soon ships sailed away
and took them to other continents to make a brand-new start,
for there are times when even sweets can taste bitter and tart.

Whelks

It was always the men who stayed behind
on the edges of our country, who gathered whelks,
searching along shorelines to see if they could find
some image of themselves; these bulky sacks
full of shells clustering in sea-pools
like small whirlwinds unstirred by tide
but remaining constant still, despite the pull
of oceans on them, washed up, discarded, left behind.

Yet despite how they seem motionless, one suspects
that they, too, travel under storm-dark waves.
Scars and fissures mark and crack their edges;
bruises black upon their surface remind us there are no safe
harbours where men can curl away from time.
It comes for us. A needle tugging life
out from where it's hidden. It will one day find
us both within dark stillness and the turbulence of light.

Unholy Mackerel

When the Sneddens started to outstay their welcome, the Macleods began to feed them mackerel.

It was a dish they rarely ate. 'A dirty fish,' Martin John's dad had called it. Like many Hebrideans of his age, he believed it shoaled in sewers or gorged on the corpses of sailors lying in sunken wrecks in the dark depths of the ocean. 'That's the reason they're so oily, all that feasting on wreckage and decay. I wouldn't give a *thank you* for one. There's some things a man shouldn't put near his mouth. Never mind in it.'

Martin John's view wasn't quite as extreme as that. He didn't really believe in all his father's legends of fish nibbling on the feet and fingers of the drowned and dead, flitting in and out of wreckage. Yet something of the old man's convictions must have stayed with him. He had no liking for mackerel. He would see them lying on the bottom of his boat, the *Mowgli,* whenever he went out fishing and would feel an involuntary shudder pass through him. There was something about the blue-grey striped back and glassy glint that did not agree with him. He even found the hard edge of its mouth repellent.

Yet here he was with his wife Sadie, beginning to serve it night after night to their visitors and smiling eagerly as if he were welcoming its presence on their plates.

'Oh, mackerel! My favourite food! The dish that Hebrideans like me most enjoy.'

He glanced over at Bill and Cynthia Snedden, two faces he had grown to loathe over the last while and tried to gauge how they were reacting to their meal. Bill sniffed a little, his features more wrinkled than ever, as if he were bemused at the nature of the dish before him. Her complexion the same silvery shade it always possessed, Cynthia looked all around the kitchen. She was obviously confused.

'Where's our knives and forks?' she asked.

❖ ❖ ❖

He remembered how it had all started. Sadie had been down in Glasgow for a gall bladder operation, resting afterwards in a small ward in the Western Infirmary. Cynthia Snedden had been in the next bed to hers, propped up on pillows with her dyed orange hair and glasses and looking at them both with a bright green gleam in her eyes. She would talk in a polite, friendly way to her Hebridean neighbours, even drawing Sadie into the conversations she was enjoying with relatives and friends who had journeyed in from the housing estate on the outskirts of the city.

'Meet ma new friends,' Cynthia would say. 'They're from a really beautiful place. Really lovely, she tells me. The farthest, distant Hebrides...'

Her granddaughter, Tiffany, would even sometimes clamber onto Sadie's bed, pushing an endless supply of illustrated children's books into her fingers, a Ladybird edition of Kipling's *Jungle Book* or *Goldilocks and the Three Bears*, perhaps, or the colourful pages of Judith Kerr's *The Tiger Who Came To Tea*.

'Read this. You gonna dae that for me?'

Sadie would oblige, reading the book slowly and carefully in a way she had never done for her own children, long grown up.

'Once there was a little girl called Sophie and she was having tea with her mummy in the kitchen. Suddenly there was a ring at the door.'

Sadie pointed to the colourful pictures – the boy surrounded by trees and creepers, the one of a tiger sitting beside Sophie at a table, a china cup brimful of tea in its claws, Daddy Bear shouting 'Who's been eating my porridge?'

'She loves your accent,' Cynthia would tell her when Tiffany had finally gone home. 'Thinks it's pure, dead brilliant.'

Bill, too, was often in the hospital, offering Martin John guidance on how to get round the city. He would be on hand when Sadie wanted him to go and buy something or other – a present for one of the neighbours back home on the island or some female item Martin John felt too embarrassed to buy.

'Get the 62 bus,' he might say, 'or take the underground.' He'd pause for a moment, look over in Cynthia's direction and nod. 'Here. I'll go with you. It must be very confusing for you to get round the city, is it no? Especially when you come from a place like the islands. Awfully easy for a man like you to get lost down here.'

There was no doubt that much of this was helpful, especially the first few times he stepped down into the Underground. Down, down, down, the endless steps seemed to go into the darkness, moving quickly past the Cal-Mac adverts with their pictures of a sunlit beach in the isle of Harris. ('Bermuda? Bahamas? St Kitts?' the words asked. 'It looks lovely. It would be really nice to go there,' Bill would say each time he encountered them.) Round, round, round sped the little orange train, passing stations with names that seemed almost identical to him in his confusion. Round, round, round went the words on Bill Snedden's lips, a constant reel of conversation in which one word was barely distinguishable from the one that followed, each statement blending with the click-clack, shake-and-rattle of the train. He was barely listening when the request came one afternoon when they stepped off the train at Buchanan Street in the city centre, his ears humming with the voices that surrounded and overwhelmed him.

'Me and Cynthia, we've never been that much up north. Never been to the Hebrides. Would you mind if we came up and stayed with you for a while? A few days or so. We wouldnae take up that much room.'

Martin John remembered looking into Bill's face and nodding.

'I'm sure we wouldn't mind that. Just for a wee while. I'm sure we wouldn't mind at all.'

❖ ❖ ❖

And that was what led to all of this – the arrival of the Sneddens just ten days or so after Sadie's return home from the hospital. Surrounded by their suitcases, the couple stood at the ferry terminal, looking out at the streets of the town, the harbour and the grey and rocky foreshore.

'Thought there was loads of sand around here,' Bill muttered. 'That's what they told us in these pictures.'

'It's not round here ... In other parts of the island.'

'Oh.' Bill nodded. 'I thought it was everywhere.'

On their arrival in the house, it was Cynthia's turn to complain. 'What about birds?' she asked. 'I thought there were loads of birds around here. I've hardly seen any since I arrived.'

'But there's plenty,' Martin John protested.

'Not as many as the pigeons you see in Glasgow. They all crowd round your feet when you walk round George Square.'

He tried to explain that to see the birds in these parts, you had to go out and look at them. They were gathering on the beaches. They were nesting on the headlands. They flew from cliffs or skerries. They did their best to avoid men rather than cluster near their toes. Despite his words, neither of the visitors listened. Bill shook his head and smiled grimly.

'I thought you teuchters were closer to nature. Not farther away.'

Neither Martin John nor Sadie spoke much after that. Not even in Gaelic – the language they spoke mostly to each other when they were on their own. (Bill had objected to that, saying it was bad manners to talk in a tongue not everyone staying in the household understood.) Instead, they could only observe as the Sneddens monopolised their home, watching a loop of soap opera and wildlife programmes on TV that seemed to circle as endlessly as the Glasgow underground. Round, round, round swam shoals of bright tropical fish flitting in and out of the hull of some sunken ship or rock. Round, round, round stepped the tiger as he crept close to his prey. And all the time, the Sneddens were sitting there eating, gorging on each snack and titbit that was in their fridge, making sure that the dinner table was empty of food.

Both he and Sadie felt more and more trapped by them.

'When will they leave?' they whispered in the darkness.

'How can we get them to go...?'

'Will they ever pay for anything themselves?'

It was in this hush that Martin John muttered his solution to the problem.

'We'll have to feed them mackerel...'

There was plenty of it to be found in the big chest freezer in the garage – the results of the many fishing expeditions when Martin John had been on the *Mowgli* and found nothing but that particular fish swimming towards his hooks and nets. There were almost as many ways to cook the fish too. They could boil or grill it, fry or curry it, even conceal its delights within a barbecue or sweet-and-sour sauce. Whispering to each other that first night, they decided that boiling was to be their first option, setting it on the table before their guests. Bill and Cynthia said nothing as they watched it lie steaming on the plate before them, joined by a couple of Kerr Pink potatoes. To begin with, they only sniffed the air, as if they were big cats sizing up an unusual prey. Eventually, Cynthia must have decided it was going to be fine; they looked around for the kitchen utensils with which they were normally provided before beginning their meal.

'Where's our knives and forks?' she asked.

'We don't use any.' Martin John smiled. 'Hebrideans always eat fish with their fingers.'

Bill sniffed once again, as if he were suspicious of the answer. 'You sure?'

'Aye. It's been that way for centuries in these parts.'

'All right then ...'

Martin John grinned contentedly as he watched them begin to eat. They pecked at first, stripping away the outside layer of skin. Daintily, they dug into the flesh, seeking to avoid the harsh spikes of both fin and bone cutting into their fingers, eyeing warily the tail that flapped lifelessly on the plate's edge. Slowly, reluctantly, they placed each bite into their mouths. Their cheeks were swollen as they chewed, doing their best not to spit the food out. They both gulped as they swallowed, as if they were in danger of choking and gagging on each mouthful sliding down their throats.

Somehow they succeeded, even possessing sufficient grace to smile when their host asked them how they had enjoyed their food.

'Well ...' Bill said.

'I suppose we could get used to it,' Cynthia smiled.

Martin John smiled once again. 'We've decided to give you the chance to do that. Tomorrow we're going to have it fried ...'

He said this with a note of triumph, knowing that if the meal did not work, there were other options over the days ahead. The following day it would be grilled. The day after that, it would be the mackerel he had taken out and stored in salt. The next meal, it might be curried. There was no doubt in his mind that he would defeat them, bringing an end to their stay.

However, when he looked at them for a reaction, there was nothing that he could see. Instead, there was the same look of bland indifference on their faces as there was when they watched their favourite wildlife programmes, seeing a tiger making its way across open grassland, a shoal of fish criss-crossing the wreck of an old sunken ship. He knew right then that he might never get them to go. They might spend the rest of their lives sitting on his sofa, eating his food and watching his TV.

Songs of an Inner Émigré

Part Two

4 ⁂ Peat Road

In summer, tractors rattle
down that track,
sending lapwings spiralling,
sheep into flight,
turning terns into a squadron
that soars and swoops to conquer
at the cough of an exhaust.

But this winter, greater stir was caused
by the revving of a solitary car
parked beside that loch
where swans congregate
like snowfall,
and the single figure found
slumped above the wheel,
face shaded blue by smoke.

5 ❧ Zuguruhe

It affects us all – the sense of restlessness
that overcomes us when we see greylags graze
on a green field in a northern isle; a flap
occurring in some hidden chamber of our hearts
reminding us that those who stay here do so at a cost,
for men remain unsettled since the day ancestors crossed
from horizon to horizon without fear of being lost.

But lost we are now – for all that we're aware
of the landscape these geese touch down on every year
to breakfast on the blades and stubble we build fences round
seeking to claim ownership of each bare patch of ground,
posts pounded in like stakes to pin and hold us down.

And we envy them their trespasses, how latitudes of light
give way to flocks that follow principles of flight;
longing to be like them, learning to accept
ourselves the way they do, the soft, bare pelt
of being human fitting snugly as feathers, down
enclosing their form, lowering and lifting them from ground
without our need to forgive ourselves, requirement also to atone

For wrongs done to one another, this planet, too, that we
share with these migrants, our hold so frail and temporary.

When he looked upon her
he didn't see suburban life, a mortgage;
all he saw was an opportunity
to step out from the cage
the island had become for him,
gaining freedom from the rage
of tempests,
a village where every thought and movement
seemed to occur on stage.

And so, when he took her to his bed,
he clasped a kind of freedom
that seemed to be inherent in her flesh
when their bodies thrashed like marram grass
that whipped them on the shore that day
their lives first fused together,
a storm that reeled him from its life,
its inclemency of weather.

Hebridean Rebel-Songs

1

Each Sunday Calum used to haunt the village road
with a sheaf of oats tucked below his arm,
pretending he had to go and tend his flock
in a false errand intended purely to alarm
the congregation on their way from kirk
all aware of this act by a neighbour
untouched by their harvest,
alone despite their prayers and labours
in a place where he was destined to remain,
clutching straw while others gathered grain.

2

John would scramble hills with fistfuls
of mica, gneiss and quartz,
sandstone or balsa some sailor was
kind enough to bring from foreign parts,
and place them on large stones, set side by side
on the summits of hills, still shorelines,
cliff-tops that veered down to meet the tide,
peaks and crests where he could go and hide
on Sundays when others went to kirk to pray.
making that the high point of their day.

3

Always restless.
Unwilling to be ruled in school.
Feet kicking at
the confines of his desk.

Always restless.
Unable to withstand work's strict demands.
Putting both his boss
and colleagues to the test.

Always restless.
Sundays never still enough to pray.
Impatient with each hour
of peace and rest.

Restless, too, within his coffin.
Some say fists hit and struck the lid,
while lips screamed out the words.
'Not yet! Oh, no! Not that time yet!'

DREAM-GLASSES
(FOR GYRDIR)

Malcolm used to wear his specs to bed
to see more clearly dreams

Turned fogged and misted after years
of troubled, restless sleep

Had blurred his night-time vision,
preventing him from visiting

Foreign ports discovered in his youth;
those sailings to Tangiers, Marseilles,

Pale women laced with perfume
in rooms he could not focus on

Till he strapped tight his glasses
and he could once more visualise

Lipstick, flesh and lingerie,
seeing, too, behind the eyes

Of all the nearby bachelors,
sharing the lost lovers

They'd let slip from tweed blankets
but returning now to haunt them

As they stretched for warmth and comfort
on dark, myopic nights.

Scenes from a Hebridean Romance

Part Three

As he fastened his tie that evening, Murray considered the fact that up until this stage in life, his voice had been his greatest weakness.

He had discovered how much power it possessed the day he travelled down the machair road in his old Vauxhall Viva with Peigi, a girl from the district. Pretty and pert with brown hair, blue eyes, and arched eyebrows that gave her face a look of perpetual surprise, she had been out with him a hundred times before. But they had mainly been in the company of her boyfriend Graham, who was away on a course on the mainland for a month or two. During his absence there had been occasional ventures into town, journeys to the local hall or pier-ends, sprints like this across the undulating green landscape of the coastline where they played games of 'hunt-the-rabbits', chasing bunnies into their burrows with the beams of their headlights.

This night, however, was different. They stopped near the edge of the local cemetery, catching occasional glimpses of the various epitaphs by flicking the headlights on and off – 'In Memory of Ebenezer MacLachlann Graham, Merchant and Bachelor of This Parish' – and listening to the whoop of the curlew and the high-pitched cries of the lapwings as they swept high above the car roof. He could hear too the surge of the sea a short distance away, like the beat of his heart breaking against the whiteness of the sands. There was something in all of this that provoked him to sing, the words of Gaelic song pure and stream-like in the awesome stillness of air.

'Apheigi, aghraidh, 's tù dh'fhàg mi buileach gun sunnd,
'S mi seoladh an-dràst' thar sàil dh'Astràilia null,
Tha 'n oidhche fluich, fuar,'s mi shuas ga cumail air chùrs'...'

She looked at him in an even more startled way than usual as
the words spilled out, surprised that this lad – Graham's ugly
friend – could sing with such beauty and grace. For a short
while afterwards she couldn't even speak, but sat there with
her eyes watering, trying to catch and control her breath, still
and steady the frenzy of her heart.

'You sang that song for me...?'

'Yes. I suppose so.'

And then her hands were all over him, stripping off the
Arran jumper his mother had knitted so lovingly, tearing the
buttons from his checked shirt to reveal the string vest below.

'Murray ... Murray...' she kept saying in between the kisses.
'That's the most beautiful thing anyone's ever done for me.'

He remembered thinking, as he saw the little white bra
with pink flowers she had on beneath her blouse, that this
was the most beautiful thing anyone had ever done for him;
more than he had ever dreamed would happen for years to
come. He had supposed he was doomed to live out much
of his life as a perpetual virgin. After all, as the mirror kept
reminding him every time he passed the fireplace of his home,
he was not the most prepossessing of young men. He had red,
round cheeks, a brown mat of hair, double chin, and narrow,
squinting blue eyes which his mother kept insisting were his
finest features. And then there was the ridiculous name that his
father had insisted on giving him when he stepped drunkenly
into the Registry Office a few days after his birth – 'Murray
Murray'. It provided yet another reason for the thousands
of bad jokes that had been directed at him during primary

school and beyond.

'Don't worry, worry. Here comes Murray Murray. He'll eat all the curry, curry. So you'd better hurry, hurry!'

Yet now there was this – the trembling and excitement caused by the touch and feel of female flesh, her nakedness pressed against his. He rejoiced in all of it, ignoring even the fact that she kept repeating his name far more often than the most unpleasant and persistent of his childhood bullies.

'Murray … Murray … Murray … Murray…'

It was only afterwards that Murray became more than a little worried about their tryst within his Vauxhall Viva. There was the fact that he couldn't even look at Graham after he returned to the island. He pretended he wasn't in the house when his old friend called on the phone, locking himself inside his bedroom wardrobe one evening rather than go downstairs to speak to him. There was the possibility of Peigi becoming pregnant. He knew only too well what happened when two people were forced to become married because of a child; his own father had left home shortly after the Incident in the Registry Office, largely – or so he claimed – because his mother wouldn't stop complaining about the choice of his son's name.

'He's called Murray Murray… And you tell me you're not worried?'

And then, there was the fact that Peigi wasn't exactly the most interesting person he had ever met, being only interested in sex and his singing voice. She would keep urging him to sing wherever he was – from the back seat of his Vauxhall Viva to a night out with her friends.

'Siuthad! Give us a song!'

He would do his best to oblige, entertaining them with a verse or two from 'Balaich an Iasgaich' or 'Fàili, faili, faili hò ro', a blast of port-à-beul. The problems really began when she asked him to sing to her French pen-friend, Eilidh Larouse, one evening. He was concerned about her response from the moment his mouth opened. As the opening words rang out,

'Tha slighe dhoirbh gu beanntan àrd ar n-eilean,
Tha 'n dìreadh garbh troimh'n mhòintich
is troimh'n fhraoich ...',

he could see a spark in her olive-green eyes, her mouth forming an endless 'O' of wonder. Her tawny skin possessed its own heightened shade too, a blush colouring her face as her breath raced and quickened.

By the time he reached the final verse, he could see her tongue dabbing the edges of her lips, her eyes becoming narrow and hooded.

'O Eilidh, ghràidh, thoir dhomh do làmh is fan rium
Far 'na bhòidich sinn's a dh'aidich sinn ar gaol ...'

She followed him into the bathroom, tugging the catch closed a few seconds after he stepped in there. He heard the swish of her Paisley pattern dress as she tugged it over her head; saw her dark hair cascading, the black bra and pants she wore below.

'Oh, Murray ... Murray ... Murray ...' she declared, 'I want you so, so much.'

Within seconds, her arms were around him, stripping him of his clothes, the Fair Isle jumper and polo shirt he was wearing on that occasion.

Within minutes there was a loud hammering outside. Peigi's demanding voice edged through the crack in the doorway.

'Murray! Murray! Murray! Are you in there?'

❖ ❖ ❖

It was a pattern that would follow him throughout his life.

His marriage to Màiri – whom he wooed with a chorus

88

or two of 'An Tèid Thu Leam, A' Mhàiri' – came to an end when he accidentally won over a woman called Jennifer with a rendition of 'Jennifer Eccles'. Morag, Lucy and Cairstìona were gained and lost in much the same way. And for all that he claimed never to want to perform the 'runaround' on 'Sue', he soon did so when a Brazilian dancer called Lola wandered near his path. Somewhere along the way, too, he lost his daughter Sylvia's mother, and Barbara Ann, the woman who gave birth to his son, Murray II.

Looking back, he thought that, for all the music that filled his life, it was an existence that lacked any harmony, ruined by his prodigious gift for song. Too often the power of his voice had helped him to make the wrong choices, relying on its pitch and power to smooth the turbulence he had created in his existence. And as a result he would gaze into his whisky glass, singing maudlin tunes to himself, searching for that sense of belonging he had never managed to possess.

It was Gormshuil who helped him find it – the only woman he had ever met whose name never suggested any rhythm or melody, only the gargling sound of someone clearing their throat. A round-faced woman with her hair wrapped tightly in a grey bun, she stepped tentatively into his home, gently removing the tumbler from his fingers.

'What would you want with that? It'll only make you feel sorry for yourself. Any fool can find a good reason to do that.'

She persisted, making a cup of tea occasionally, a meal or two. At first, he spat in fury when she suggested going to church with him, turning on her when she came into his home.

'What would I want to go there for?'

But her words had led to tonight – the way he had tightened his tie a thousand times that evening, preparing to go out to the front of the church and lead the congregation in singing the psalms. He held the psalmody tightly in his hand, waiting to hear the minister announce his choice of psalm.

'O thigibh, seinneamaid do Dhia,
Thigibh gach neach na làthair...'

'O come, let us sing to the Lord,
Come let us everyone...'

His voice rang out as clearly as it had done that first night he sang to Peigi on the machair, gathering and becoming part of all the riches he had heard that day. The whoop of the curlew as it flew, its wings beating below the swirl of the galaxies above, the fixed beam of the Pole Star in the darkness of the heavens. The swirling cries of the lapwing as they performed their aerobatics just outside the range of his car headlights. The glorious stillness of the planet as the waves beat against the beach, echoing the drumming of his pulse. The words filled his mouth as if he was calling out against eternity and its endless, relentless ability to perform wicked jokes on men, to wash the meaning of their lives away.

And he looked up from his book to see the women gazing at him. Gormshuil, Agnes, Raonaid sitting in their pews. A smile was on all their faces, a full flush of colour shading their pale and wrinkled skins.

OLD SPINSTERS

In my youth, I was surrounded by a multitude of Miss
                                        Havishams,
though somewhat in reverse – for they were garbed in funeral dress
since the day their fathers, mothers, sisters, brothers
passed away, as if flesh was forced to take on black
to accompany their lost souls as they stepped into the dark.

Their clocks stopped too, preserving in grim perpetuity
their fidelity to lost ones who were gone
with their passing marked by donning of black skirt and
                                        cardigan.
A uniform of death that marked far more than any headstone
signs that those they loved and cared for were all they
                                        thought upon.

OLD BACHELORS

And Magwitch too. These grey-clothed men
with grey skin, hair and talk,
hobbled by these leg-irons
fastening them to islands
to which they keep returning,
never learning how true comfort's rare
within such borders. Instead the bare,
scarce speech of bar-rooms where
nightly talk comes round
to how life might have been less bitter
if their feet had not been bound
by these shackles that confined them
to this narrow slip of ground.

NOSTALGIA

Though I stroll beside still waters that sweep through Babylon,
let me not forget the waves that rampage near my home,

The breakers thundering on rocks at Cladach Dibadale,
the spume that spikes and troughs on far Sgeir Dhail

On quiet evenings, echoing in the ears of men
driving sheep out the Aird road or down towards the glen,

Staying with them like a cloud or veil of sound
thick as the cloak of midges that followed them around.

Let me not forget either how strong men often wept
With home-sickness as dreams in exile kept

Reminding them of Asmigarry, Rathad Ùr, Buaile na Crois,
all that they had forsaken, surrendered, lost

That day they stepped outside the boundaries of home,
exchanging that bare landscape for the halls of Babylon.

If things got worse, he could always force
himself, without compunction or remorse,
to curse his superior in the work-place, divorce
his wife, and after being made homeless, return again
                                        to source
to follow in the stride and step of ancestors
performing tasks they'd done for centuries before
like cutting peats for fuel out on the moor
or scavenging for flotsam washed up on the shore.

If things got worse, he could always seek
alternative income, now the economy looked bleak,
by lifting winkles, developing his physique
pounding fence-posts on the machair week after
                                        mindless week,
embarking on a programme where he set aside
the certificates and salary in which he once took pride
to exist without the megabucks he'd long needed to survive,
cutting through his credit-card with the quick slash
                                        of a knife.

If things got worse, he could always live
on sea-pink, heather, the sprawl and tuck of fish
hooked upon the foreshore, all that was in the gift
of the old world that he'd squandered and let slip.

SONGS OF RESIDENCE

1 DRIVING THROUGH THE DISTRICT

Seeking to turn our small world topsy-turvy,
we would twist the village signposts back to front
or wrong way round, lengthening the stay
of those who strayed among us during winter months,

Granting them a set of unexpected corners,
zigzags and cul-de-sacs they'd failed to see before:
the lighthouse lit and lifted far down south,
the graveyard shifting out from shore to moor,

Till each mile began to baffle and bewilder
with unfamiliar landmarks, unsuspected sights,
and they could no longer make out near from far,
the stillness of the moor from shifting tide;

Our island stretching to hold nations
with some swearing, as they passed by the Hall,
that they had just seen the Champs d'Elysées
while one man said he'd glimpsed the Taj Mahal.

Wonders might have crossed that ground
on days when deaf or dumb ones kneeled to pray
for sound to be restored or those born blind to share
their first glimpse of the Church in Eoropie,

Or that Easter dark clouds tumbled,
bringing snow that levelled cairn and grass,
coaxing me out from the fireside
to stand and see a marvel come to pass;

A lamb my uncle dug out from the snow.
Holding its frozen body in his grasp,
I watched breath rise and steam from lips to nose,
and life return – small gasp by shuddering gasp.

Longships looped rope through that eye
waves had drilled in Lewisian gneiss

and tried to drag the island past
inlets and headlands, the still mass

of the mainland – its people looking on askance
as moor and machair shifted stance

with Callanish unearthed and uprooted, Uig's
hills torn from foundations, responding to the tug

of prow and stern, seafarers' strong arms
whose grip began to fumble when alarm

boomed and hollered from the south
with warnings passed from mouth to trembling mouth

that sand and stone were starting to resist
their efforts. New islands – Barra, Vatersay, Uist –

began a fresh existence, breaking from the whole
till even Harris almost slipped from hold

of Norsemen determined after years
abroad to take rock home as souvenir

of time spent south. Their grip grew loose
and hopeless. One untied the noose,

concluding that despite their sweat and strain,
islands could not shift and would remain

firmly in that wild, wet space
their old Gods had determined they were placed.

Some October evenings we used to slip
across barbed wire to steal turnips,
ripping stalk and leaves, taking time to strip

Roots free from soil. Then we'd shed
purple-peel in mock-hurry to be fed
on gains our night-time raids had furnished.

One time we were caught. Our faces burned
with guilt and fear's delirium,
glowing like Hallowe'en lanterns

With round eyes, wide slits
like gaping mouths our blades had chipped
from that season's crop we loved to nick.

5 ← FUNERAL PASSING CROSS PRIMARY SCHOOL

More than the chant of catechism, prayer, psalm,
there was the chilling sense of calm
with which we watched that line outside the gates;
those men in dark suits passing on the weight
of death to one another, hand over hand
on that rail with the slow rhythm of a dance
we knew we'd have to partner some fine day.
A few kept glancing. Others turned away.
Some did sums, concentrating as if they
were adding totals of both doubt and faith
to find which side of these lines their answers lay.
A shoulder shrug or anxious words of prayer.
Fearful calculations continuing until
clock ticked on and hearse heaved up the hill.

Scrape a shoe and you can read
that island's landscape.

The underlay of peat
etched deep within its sole.

A twist of heather snarled
and fastened in its laces

The green shade of croftland
colouring seams that stitch together

Its old and battered leather,
like fine lines connecting

Sharp cuts of moor and shore.
That shoe recalls for me

Times when life seemed on its uppers
and I kicked clouds of sand

Wanting to plunge my feet in salt
and wade my way through water,

Seeking to find a place where toes
might not be bruised or broken

And the narrowness of eyelets
could look at far horizons

And see tracks where feet could stride across
and both heel and toe might stand.

Gulls have large, strong hearts
disproportionate to body size,
hollow bones
and relentless appetites

I imagined might just
gorge on me
when they gathered on the moor,
a sniping, biting colony

Lifting and rippling
on each furl of air
in strong and shredding waves
that seemed at times to dare

To break upon my bootsteps
as I watched them dumb of words,
imagining them rehearsing
for bit-parts in Hitchcock's *Birds*

I'd peeked at some darkened midnight,
shrinking deep within my seat,
its terrors more convincing
with each relentless beat

Of these sturdy, scavengers' wings,
huge and ravenous hearts,
each reel of film in which I
was forced to play a part.

8 Ness Social Club, Fivepenny Machair
(NEAR THE BUTT-OF-LEWIS)

Beer foamed like the near Atlantic
when we sat in that bar
which you – my city friend –
declared was the nearest
that you'd ever come
to this world's farthest end.

And these words made me think,
for between throatfuls of drink
I swallowed there
were times I heard
Shonnie speak of Sydney,
Murdo muttering of Mexico
and Donnie talking about years ago
when he'd spent days in Durban,
Hamburg, Tokyo.

The whole world spun
till I could see
huge and red at nightfall
sun
slipping down the window,
out of reach
as it spilled a thousand colours
on machair, wave and beach.

And it wasn't just drink talking
when I swirled down my beer
and said, 'The farthest end?
The world could find its centre here.'

Joe and Biddy will not be sitting by the Rayburn
waiting for your return.

Their children born in your absence will not be given your name,
but – you will learn – be called 'Titania', 'Margherita', 'Oberon'

In honour of the TV in the corner
constantly switched on.

Let not your mouth froth in anticipation
of foods that were once familiar,

But expect instead lasagne, chicken korma,
for the Scotch broth you once savoured has long gone

And has been substituted by other sustenance
from horizons you have sometimes stepped along.

So come back with small expectations
from New York, Paris, London, Munich,

Whatever shore your life has chanced upon.
Years have passed;

Though you came to earth on this landscape,
you no longer quite belong.

Scenes of Death in the Hebrides

1᛭ Sheep-Shears

The old sheep-shears have come to life, those kept within the barn.
They're all trembling and clicking. Perhaps someone ought
to warn
people that they're coming and are out to cause them grievous
harm.
The old sheep-shears have come to life, the ones kept within
the barn.

The old sheep-shears have come to life, those for clipping wool
off the backs of black or white sheep, some thirty-three bags full,
but they're no longer used to snip them or keep these
creatures cool.
The old sheep-shears have come to life, the ones for shearing wool.

The old sheep-shears have come to life and they're coming
after you
for not following father's footsteps, finding other things to do,
and they'll clip away your trouser-crotch to let wind and sleet
blow through.
The old sheep-shears have come to life and they're coming
after you.

2 PEAT-BLADE

Those hours upon the peat-bank
must have been the only time
he granted power to her

when he bowed bare head
to lift up oozing slabs
of peat for fire

and she held in her hands
the shaft of wood
knowing, if she wanted, that she could

with sharp edge
at his fingers,
gash his flesh

and watch blood gush
from skin.
A sudden act of vengeance

for all the years
she'd suffered wounds
from him.

The day it first said Saddleworth,
she had a vision of that mound of earth
they'd dug out on the island moor, herself and her big sister.
These steps they'd scrambled by the river
in winter's dark when secrets the pair of them had hidden
let slip news of their existence, kicked and wrestled from within,
and how she'd whispered word that breath was stirring
through pursed lips in their kitchen,
each consonant and vowel mingling with the coruscating pain
that bowed her as they staggered out in unforgiving rain.

So much so long forgotten, interred
like all the faded promise of these words
he'd used to coax her down upon her back
in machair grass or shade of haystack
that summer just before he was called up for
the putting on of uniform to prepare for foreign war.

So much so long forgotten, though all that time was stored
in the silence that stays hidden behind a spinster's door,
in peat with which she nursed her household's flames,
in the Bible grave and weighty with her shame,
in kitchen clocks that so remorselessly tick,
in the wireless that intruded with its talk of politics,

Until the hour it spoke of Brady, Hindley,
when the spirits of these children would not let her be
but rose and peopled silence,
the haunts that all those dead from violence
are doomed to shade and patronise
till she saw out from the bank he slept in, rise

that child she half-hated and half-loved
stand up in accusation from his cloak of peat and turf
to chant the names of those who had lain by his side –
'Pauline Reade, Keith Bennett, John Kilbride...'

GUTTING-KNIFE

How did you find that knife?

It was shoved in the back of a drawer in my granny's bedroom.
I came across it – all wrapped up in an old tartan shawl – when
me and Mam were cleaning the house after she died. There were
a lot of things in there. A rusty locket. Some faded postcards.
Letters from home. A couple of old pictures of women standing
over barrels of fish, dressed in their aprons and things. That
notebook I was telling you about.

Oh, yes. What was in that notebook?

It was some kind of diary. One that she must have written when
she was working away from home. Accounts of her days in
places like Lerwick, Wick, Aberdeen, even Lowestoft. Following
the herring, I think she called it. Lots of girls from the islands
did that way back then when they were young and unmarried.
Looking for money for themselves and their families.

Did you sit down and read it right away?

No. Not right away. It was the knife that got my attention first
of all. I remember my mam saying when I found it: 'Trust that
bitter old witch to keep something like that.' She had no time
for her mam. Just like I had little time for her. Perhaps that's the
kind of thing that runs in certain families. Carried in the genes.
Hatred and spite. Like other people inherit blue eyes, long noses,
black hair from one another. Our lot inherit anger and dislike.

(Pause)

I've forgotten the question.

That's all right, Isobel. You said you didn't read the notebook right away. When did you?

About a week after I took it home. I opened up the shawl and found the notebook and gutting knife inside it. That was weird, especially when I was sure I had thrown the knife in the bin. It was then, too, I began to read what she had written. And after I did that, there was no stopping me. I looked over it – again and again – night after night for weeks on end.

And what was in it?

Well, it started off quite normally. It just told how sad she was leaving her family in the village and heading off to the mainland. She mentioned her friends too. One called Katag, who came from down the district. Another with the name of Murdag who was – according to my granny – 'as daft as a watch you could buy for a penny'. She wrote, too, about the places they stayed in, what conditions were like for the girls, what food they ate, how they slept and kept themselves clean. How their backs ached after standing for hours on end every day half-bent over these huge catches of fish. How they all smelled of herring, unable to get the stink of fish out of their clothes and skin. Even a couple of jokes and laughs they all shared. How Murdag tried to bite into an orange without removing the peel. And then the whole thing changed...

How did it do that?

It started to be mainly about the knife. How she got it from this strange looking Shetlandman who had just about thrust it into her hand. 'Tak dis, lass,' he had said. 'Hit's a guid, sharp blade. Hit'll cut weel for da liks of dee.' And then he ran off in the direction of the town centre, long before she had the chance to speak. After that, a page or so later, there was this

110

long description of the knife, one that went on for ages and ages.

Sorry?

It was weird, obsessive stuff. Page after page of it. She wrote about how it balanced perfectly in her hand, fitting snugly in her fingers. She mentioned this cherry-red mark on its handle, wondering if it were a bloodstain that no one could clean. There was this hook, too, just the right shape and position – she said – for her thumb. A little red there, too, on its underside that she couldn't remove. And then there was the blade. She described that in detail. The manufacturer's name – 'I. Frinn' – printed faintly on its side. The little curved hook at its tip. The scratches along the surface of the steel. A flawless knife, she called it. A perfect tool for her trade. And then, there was almost boasting. How many herring she could gut in a single day. The seamless way she could draw her knife across the stomachs of these fish, removing the long trail of blood and guts with one gash. How it could chop a herring's head off from the remainder of its body, cutting it off with one sharp jerk of the blade. How, too, it would never cut her – not like the other girls whose hands were full of nicks and scratches, no matter how hard they tried to protect their hands by wrapping them in tattered bandages. How despite that the salt would get into their skin, turning each wound red and sore and angry. She had none of this. And what was more…

(Pause)

Yes?

The curers began to notice her. The big businessmen who swaggered around the quayside with their hands in their pockets, sizing up the girls and their work. One or two would gather round as she stood in her oilskin apron, gutting her way through the multitude of fish the drifters had brought to shore. 'Aye,' they would say, 'she's a grand worker, that one. The best lassie for the gutting that I've ever seen.' Sometimes – so my gran would say – they'd give her an extra few pennies for her efforts. 'Got to keep a good quine like you content,' they'd smile. And then she started getting attention of a sort that she didn't really appreciate so much.

When did that happen?

On the quayside at Wick. A man called Gunn kept a close eye on her there. Much too close for her liking. He'd stand behind her at the barrels. Rub himself against the folds at the back of her skirt. 'You're doing a great job there, girlie,' he would say, 'but I keep on wondering if there's any other uses we could put these nimble fingers to ...' And then he even took her hand – all flecked with silver scales and blood – and placed it against his crotch. 'I know these hands can do a great job, but I've a funny feeling your thighs would do an even better one.'

(Pause)

She wasn't the only one he was behaving like that to. There were others too. Sniffing round them all the time. Seeing if he could get anything out of them. His wicked way. Mr Gunn, they would joke, the man with his fingers always on his trigger. But they were scared of him too. After all, they were strangers in his country. It wasn't as if they were safe at home. If they said anything, there was the chance they would not be believed. 'Och, you teuchter girls. You're always good with the stories.'

Did she write how she felt about that?

Aye. But in a very strange way. 'The knife felt good in my hand today. Neat and trim and deadly. As if I give control to it, allowing it to take over my fingers, making my hand go fast or

112

slow or gentle. Directing the dip and flow of my arm. Working out the weight or lightness of my touch. Cut. And the fish's belly is split open. Cut. Chaidh baga Gunn a reubadh. Cut. And the fish's head is tossed aside. Cut. Chaidh bàrr a'bhoid a shàthadh. We are all happy the man has been stripped of his roe.'

And then?

Nothing. You tell me that in the papers of the time there's reports of a man called Daniel Gunn who's gone missing. Never to be seen again. But there's no mention of that in her notebook, only that she's having these terrible dreams. All about her work. How her gutting knife is taking over more and more of her existence. How she wakes in the middle of the night with her hand frenzied and unable to lie still. How she finds these marks across her stomach, as if she has slashed herself with her own blade.

Nothing about her time getting treatment in the hospital at Craig Dunain?

No. You've told me that. How the girls from the district took her to the doctor. How she spent over a year getting treatment for her troubles. Nothing about any of that. Only two more sentences about the knife. 'I have put it in the back of the drawer. It will stay there forever.'

Till you took it out?

Aye. And in the months that followed, I had time to do it more and more. Examining it. Balancing it in my fingers. Noting its inscription, its cherry red stain, little scratches on the steel. Seeing how that little hook fitted my thumb too. Perfectly and neatly. Using it to open envelopes. Chopping meat and vegetables with it. Using its blade to draw furrows across my skin. Storing it in my handbag when I went out on the razzle at the weekend.

113

Until that day your mother started at you?

Yeah. Nagging on at me about how I should go out and look for a job. How I was drinking and moping around too much. And I remember arguing with her. How I couldn't be expected to go back to work in an office where a man like Groper Gillies was in charge, with his hand always ready to slip up a girl's skirt or touch her boobs. And she said, 'Perhaps you shouldn't go around dressing the way you do then, putting temptation in the man's way.' And that's when I took the knife out. Fished it from the bottom of my handbag. And even as I did that, it seemed to take control of my fingers. I held it tightly in my fist and stepped in her direction, feeling it shove and thrust my arm...

Haunted by Joe Strummer

The Sound of Raasay calling till
he's standing out in ancestral
haunts his granddad must have known,
like Suidhisnis or Screapadal,
Caolas Rònaidh, surroundings where hazel,
birch or rowan have long grown,

And now thrash to break the peace of Sabbath
or prohibit strangers from the path
to Umachan where a roofless house
offers up a gable to provide
shelter to those restless ones who stride
towards it across bracken, heather, moss,

To a ruin where a guitar thunders in his hands
bringing songs as adamant and jagged as that land
once cleared of his kin,
a hammering of rain and mist
drumming hard his pleas for justice,
clouds clashing high on Dun Caan and the Westway for him.

HAUNTED BY MARVIN GAYE

Headlines – not the grapevine – let me know
that sweet voice
had been pistol-cracked
by a father's reverend hand.

Soul scorched
by faith and flame,
life swinging
between mission hall and Motown,
till that hour
bullets from a .38
spat fire into his heart.

And I thought of all those I had known
– let us call them Abraham, Martin, John –
the riotous sons of righteous men
whose early years were trapped within the Bible's text
till each bond had been broken
in their teens;
the first suck of a cigarette
smoke-signalling rebellion
that soon blazed through their bodies
with the heat of drink or drugs.

Then those croft, small-town or inner-city blues,
the confusion of that question
'What's going on?'
as these spirits split by God and Satan
searched for mercy,
finding none as their lives twisted
between pub and prayer-house,
the sweet conflicting ecstasies of psalm and sex and sin.

Let that voice sing witness
to their struggle;
each note a sound that soars and falls,
mimicking journeys
of those grounded in the gospel and its songs
whose full flight crashed to land
in the shadows of a bed-sit,
a drunken accident,
or stretched out before a father,
love almost iced to hate,
his good hand reaching out
for bread-knife or Kitchen Devil,
chill of axe or hammer,
the sear of Smith & Wesson .38.

Scenes of Hebridean Haunting

Part Two

A short time after the old chief died, the cave began to draw Leod to its opening.

He could hear its voices echo as he played his music in the Great Hall, practising airs he knew the new chief, away on the mainland, never wanted to hear. That young man was down in the city, playing cards and sipping brandy while around him the young ladies, dressed in their fashions, danced and glittered all night. On the rare occasions he came home, he could be overheard humming snatches of waltzes and short refrains from some strange medley of noises he called the operetta, foreign tunes that his old father would never have allowed to tremble for a moment on his lips.

Still Leod continued to play, his fingers slipping over notes as he rehearsed a reel, lament or strathspey for his invisible audience. Someday, he convinced himself, the young chieftain would return to his homeland. Someday the remnants of the blood of his ancestors that still moved through his veins would be stirred by the ceòl-mòr. His feet would tap to its rhythms as his father's and grandfather's had done for years before him.

Yet as the months and years went on and there was less and less sign of the young chieftain ever spending any time in his island home, Leod began to grow less and less certain that such a return would ever happen. Slowly, the piper began to realise that he no longer felt comfortable playing his tunes in the Great Hall. The pictures of past chieftains and the heads of old stags seemed only to mock both him and his music, becoming the only audience he possessed. Even the hills surrounding its walls boomed in silence. He no longer felt at home there. The place where he had lived and made music for years had begun to feel alien and strange.

He began to dream of other places where he could play, recalling a cave he had discovered way out in the hills when he was young. Leod remembered how he'd stumbled across it while he had been out at the old àirigh his family had owned. Just after leaping down the face of a peat bank, he had seen that there was a gap at the foot of a stone cliff nearby, obscured partly by bracken and heather. He made his way towards it, pushing back the thick undergrowth that hid it from view.

And there it was – a split in the stone large enough for a grown man to go through. He stepped into it, conscious of a gleam sparkling in the darkness, the grey rock of its walls. Brushing it with his fingers, he was aware, too, of how it opened up after the thin crack of the entrance, becoming almost as large as the Great Hall within. Even the way his breath echoed underlined this, telling him this was no small place, but one that seemed to reach out into the dim impenetrable depths of the earth. He stepped warily within it, feeling a tumble of stones beneath his feet. As he did so, he became aware of the cave's glow becoming brighter, surrounding him with a speckled light that resembled the glistening of gold.

'Trobhad,' he heard a voice say. 'Come in...'

'Siuthad...' another urged. 'Do it...'

It was then he heard a babble of female voices, each one calling on to him to obey. They seemed to do this in a vast range of languages. Gaelic. Norse. Pictish. For a moment, he felt inclined to listen to their commands, going further and further into the cave. There seemed both warmth and welcome in its depths...

But then his footsteps stilled; his courage faltered. His foot seemed to pause in mid-stride for an age before he turned around and ran.

He had been frightened then, terrified of the unknown and the darkness, even of the shimmer of its walls. But over the years he had realised there was nothing to be scared of. The words he had heard had been comforting, gentle in the way they called upon him to step into the cave. Now, on restless nights, he heard them once again. They had soft and soothing voices, ones that caressed him when he was sleepless, drawing gently around him like fingers brushing against skin. They had all the tenderness and eagerness of the young wife he had lost twenty years before, the one whose absence he still felt from his bed.

'Trobhad … Siuthad … Thig a steach…'

The morning came when he rose up to obey them. With his bagpipes on his shoulder, Leod made his way across the moorland, playing the music of the immortals – a slow and sad lament – as he went…

❖ ❖ ❖

The old woman had long since tired them out with her talk.

This had grown much worse since the rest of the islanders had decided to move into the new houses the landlord had built. Roofs bare of thatch, they stood in a row with their doors and windows facing the open mouth of the harbour – the ideal place for their residents to look out for visiting yachts and boats sailing across the Atlantic towards them.

'They're in the wrong place,' Mag told them the day she refused to move from the stone walls of her old home. 'You'll all be proved fools for giving up your old houses. Just wait and see if I'm right.'

Things became worse when she was proved to be telling the truth. The felt roofs of the new houses were lifted up by the fierceness of the storms that funnelled through the entrance of the bay, and the villagers were unable to repair them if they were ripped or torn. Smoke swirled through their two rooms when the wind blew in the wrong direction. The inside of each window was damp with condensation.

'Well...?' she asked them.

They never answered her directly, just muttered out of the edge of their mouths.

'She can see into the future. What else could you expect from a witch?'

'Who knows where she gets that knowledge from?'

There were also the old songs and stories she kept talking about endlessly: verses about birds like the wren that were distinctive to the island, or a golden cave in a place across the sea; tales, too, of the woman who had once lived on its empty east coast and hunted deer and mythical beasts throughout the Hebrides. Once they had thrilled to them. Nowadays, they were only interested in psalms and tales from the Bible. They shook their heads dismissively each time she mentioned them.

'We spoke about these things when we were ignorant and foolish. We have learned since then.'

Eventually, they decided they had endured Mag long enough. They went to the hovel she called home one moonlit night and bundled the old witch out its door. Their mouths hissed at her in the shadows, noting with disgust her long tangle of grey hair, the wrinkles that wove and patterned every inch of her parched and aged skin.

'We've had enough of you and your stories,' they declared. 'We want you to get out of here.'

'Why?'

'You do not belong here any more. There is no longer a place for the likes of you.'

They took her down to the harbour where a boat was waiting. Slowly, surely, they took her away from the island where she had lived all her days, heading east to the places where the remainder of the world's people stayed, their oars dipping rhythmically in the calm, still sea. She looked at them with the same haunted quality as the moon above their heads, demanding answers to another set of questions.

'How can you say I do not belong there? I have lived there all my life.'

'The place has changed,' they answered. 'You are no longer fit to stay among us.'

'Eeesht... And where are you taking me instead?'

'Oh, anywhere. Into exile... Just as far away from the rest of us as we can possibly manage.'

'We'd row you all the way to Australia if we had the chance,' one of them scoffed.

'Leave me where the cave of gold is,' she asked them.

'What?' Their laughter was as choppy and scornful as the waves around them. 'There's no such place.'

She shook her head scornfully. 'Can you not recall the song?'

'Yes, but it's not real.'

'You sure about that?'

'Yes.'

It was her turn to laugh. She felt glad to be leaving them and all their certainties – about the new houses they had moved into; their dislike of all the old songs and stories that crossed her lips. They had built walls they could hide behind, seeking to protect themselves from all the old wonders of the world.

'Then you can leave me where the cave is meant to be?'

They looked at one another for a moment in the darkness, unable to depend on their own judgement before coming to a decision. Once again, she felt contempt for the new breed of men that surrounded her on the island. They seemed incapable of thinking for themselves. They had to rely all the time on each other. That and the Book that seemed to have deprived them of judgement.

'Oh, all right,' they finally declared. 'I don't suppose it'll do any harm.'

Her broken teeth came together in a smile. She was thinking of the piper and how his music would reverberate within the walls of the cave. It was said that the purest of notes rang out among its stones, creating the most wondrous sound that those who encountered it had ever heard. It could sometimes be heard upon the surface of the land, rippling in its lochs and streams, resounding on the moorland. Those who heard would be puzzled by its presence, wondering where it came from. All they knew was that its faintest echo washed away the grief and sadness that clung to the flesh and bones of the living. It restored youth and beauty to those who had bent and cracked beneath the weight of years.

It was then she opened her mouth and sang, her voice strengthening as the boat moved slowly towards the islands that lay on the edge of the mainland of Scotland, knowing she was on her way to a place where she might be content forever.

'Nach truagh mi Rìgh, gun trì làmhan,
Dà laimh sa phìob, dà làimh sa phìob,
Nach truagh a Rìgh, gun trì làmhan,
Da làimh sa phìob's làmh sa chlaidheamh…'

'Oh Lord, I wish I had three hands,
Two hands for the pipes, two hands for the pipes,
Oh Lord, I wish I had three hands,
Two hands for the pipes, and one for the sword…'

Mag shook her head when she thought of the words. They were about a piper who had been enticed by a monster into the Cave of Gold. He had mourned the fact that he didn't have another hand, one that might be free to fend off the great beast with the edge of his blade. She laughed bitterly and muttered to herself that it had been easy for him. No blade could perform the task she wanted to do.

The monster, after all, had long fled the cave. It was now out and about. Its spirit had entered the hearts and minds of her own people instead.

◈ ◈ ◈

There have been others joining them over the last few years.

They would land on the foreshore in their boats or reach that remote part of the moorland through a long and endless tangle of roads. They would walk then, passing a ruined airigh on their way, climbing upwards to that place they had heard existed only in songs and legends. Some would find the cave there, seeing, like the piper before them, a small cleft in the rock that they could squeeze their way through, stepping into a cave where they could be surrounded by grey walls shining with a rich seam of undiscovered gold, hearing the voices beckon to them, offering them a comfort they could not find anywhere in the modern world that had surrounded them before.

'Trobhad ... Siuthad ... Thig a-steach...'

They were a strange people who had gathered there. They included those with the richest, finest Gaelic, a depth of vocabulary that all of their friends and neighbours had lost a few generations before. There were those, too, who had skills no one in their surroundings valued any more. The man who could make a scythe sing as he swung its blade through high grass. The girl who could turn coarse wool into the finest thread on her spinning wheel. Those, too, who had never exchanged a wall of finely judged and balanced stone for a coil of barbed wire or the sweep of fence. The ones who had never lost their old trades or surrendered to the new.

And even now, they sing together in the darkness, learning

the music the first arrivals brought with them to that place.
The tunes of the piper.
Songs about the wren and countless other birds.
The innumerable stories of the cave.

EQUILOGUE

Scenes from the Existence of a Hebridean Colt

At one time, the loch formed the full extent of my pasture. I would graze in its depths, step through its shallows, raising my head only occasionally to trouble the water's surface and see what was happening on land. It was one of these times I saw Calum Seonag coming in my direction. His feet were wayward, stumbling over tussocks while he sang a tuneless version of 'Ailein Duinn' as he swaggered home.

'Mas e 'chluasag dhut a' ghaineamh
Mas e leabaidh dhut an fheamainn
Mas e 'n t-iasg do choinnlean geala
Mas e na ròin do luchd-faire…'

'If it is thy pillow the sand
If it is thy bed the seaweed
If it is the fish thy candles bright
If it is the seals thy watchmen…'

My peace disturbed, I stepped out of the water and waited for him beside the loch's edge. He was mumbling and muttering to himself, speaking of his ungrateful wife and children at home.

'They couldn't care less about me… They couldn't give a damn…'

I barely listened to his words, knowing that such ramblings took up a good share of Calum's mind. Too often his complaints echoed in the ripples of the loch, lapping again and again on its banks. Mostly, I just thought of his talk as being like the lapwing or curlew's cries, an echo from a long-forgotten, dry side of the world. This was the first time, however, I had been on land when he marched in the loch's direction. I took in at a glance the cut of him, his shirt-tail hanging out of his trousers, dark hair unkempt, blue eyes staring. His mouth was dangling so loosely, it barely allowed him to squeeze his question out.

'I need a ride home... Will you take me?'

I stepped a little nearer the loch, shying from his words, his faltering footsteps as he stumbled towards me.

'I can't walk any more...'

There was no point in shaking my mane at him. When he moved in my direction, I allowed him to clamber upon my back and to sit there.

'Giddy up... Take me home...'

Reluctantly, I turned in the direction he wanted me to take, conscious that this was the first time anyone had been perched upon me since the hour I had carried my mother and father for their final journey into the waters of the loch. As he dug his heels into my side, I recalled how my feet had moved so quickly that day, the fine brush of my tail thrashing back and forth as I thundered across moorland, stirring the corpses of the lost ones that were buried deep within its surface, disturbing their rest.

Calum Seonag kept singing more words from the same song I had heard from his lips before.

'Dh'òlainn deoch ge b' oil le càch e
De dh'fhuil do chuim 's tu 'n déidh do bhàthadh...'

'I would drink, though all would detest it,
of your heart's blood after your drowning...'

He broke off then, muttering the words 'Faster, faster...' into my ear. I decided not to listen to him, wondering why I should consider moving more quickly for this drunken fool. I would only be bringing him back to a wife and children who were probably far more content without his presence in the room, his drunken lurch and stumble into bed. Instead, I continued at my usual pace, stepping carefully over the uneven surface of the land with that burden on my back. He kept pitching back and forth, his fingers digging into me as he tried his best to stay on.

'Come on... Get a move on...'

Finally I obeyed, turning in the direction of the loch as I did so. His fingers clasped more tightly onto my mane. His feet dug harder into my side. It made no difference to my progress.

'Hey! Turn round! You're heading the wrong way. You're...'

Anxiety filled his voice. He yelled and cried as I picked up speed, recalling how it had felt when I had taken my last cargo to their deaths. And all the time I was thinking how, for all that his wife and children might cry the following morning, there would be relief mingled with their tears. There would be a release from his drunken tyranny, his shouts and rages when something went wrong with his existence, the petty rules with which he governed the household.

And as a result of that, I felt only exhilaration as the water rose up over my haunches, returning to the element where I had long belonged.

❖ ❖ ❖

After that, the full extent of my pastures began to expand a little.

I would step into the waters of other lochs, knowing that someone tired or drunk was about to come towards its edge, offering them a ride upon my back. Unaware of the destination I had planned for them, they accepted the lift gladly, only beginning to clutch my mane desperately when I moved faster, taking them towards the dark and hidden depths nearby. I would wait, too, near the banks of a larger river, grazing there until a passer-by had the mad notion of making his or her way across its currents perched upon my back. Halfway across and I'd suddenly rear up, bucking the rider from his high seat and plunging him into the quickest current, the deepest pool I could

131

find within its course.

Later, I even started to haunt the ocean, concealing myself within the dark foliage of a kelp forest growing tall and strong from the bones of small children lost or cast away on rock or sand. When a storm broke out, I'd leap from the crests of waves, merging with them in their fury, each quick and unholy squall. I'd pound on the decks of fishing boats with my hooves, bite and snap off masts with a sudden, fierce clench of my teeth. And then I'd carry the souls of men on my back, lifting them up among spume before casting them down into the depths, racing towards the shoreline.

It was on one of the nights when the Atlantic overspilled that I discovered there was much within me that was still human. White seas bombarded the ship, the *Centaur* sailing across to America. They plunged the vessel into darkness, breaking bow and stern with their weight as they had earlier cracked and shattered the stillness of the ocean. And, of course, I added to the thunderous nature of the storm, my hooves sparking off steel, my teeth splintering wood.

It was then a woman was washed from its deck. I took her as my cargo, feeling her fingers probe my neck, tangling with my mane. The sea continued to crash against her, chill seeping through her bones. It wasn't long before her grip started to loosen and I became aware that I was carrying one more rider on her passage out of existence. My task done, I rode more slowly, laying her down almost tenderly on the soft sand of the shoreline.

Her bloodless, waterlogged beauty moved me as she lay there. A slender woman in her early twenties with her dress ripped and torn by the smack of wind and wave, she looked both lovely and fragile. I could see the swell of her breast, white, delicate skin, the intense blue shade of her eyes, even the redness of her lips. And there was, too, her long red hair billowing

132

around her, shifted back and forth by the breeze.

I must confess I fell in love with her. It was an odd, giddying feeling – a mingling of lust for the softness of her flesh and a longing to see her alive again. I couldn't bear to think of the seabirds thronging, picking out her eyes and plucking at her entrails. Neither did I want to hear the bark and clamour of seals as they tore flesh from her bones. It was this thought that made me scrape up sand to cover her body. Perhaps then her red hair would merge with the kelp and her corpse would become a brown quilt of seaweed. Perhaps her beauty could be preserved from the devastation so often done by waves.

◆ ◆ ◆

That moment set me off on other journeys.

I would graze in the vicinity of other lochs and bays in the hope of coming across someone like my poor, drowned girl. I could be seen on the edges of villages and small harbours, hoping that if I waited there long enough I would see someone with her slim form, her glorious crown of red hair, that air of grace that she possessed even after the last breath of air escaped her.

For a long time I failed to do this, seeing instead a host of other women. Small, lively, brown-haired girls who talked endlessly gathering on the quayside. Wisps of girls with fine, fair hair cascading as they worked within fields close to shore. Brunettes with broad hips and shoulders tending sheep and cattle. Each one might have had some appeal for me, but I resisted, recalling the slimness of the dead girl's shoulders, the halo of her breast revealed by the torn top of her dress, the tangled tresses of her red hair. None of them could compare to the beauty I had seen that day. It belonged to her alone like the soft hush of a prayer, words of worship whispered from an angel's lips. Nothing else left me as weak and breathless as that sight.

This changed the day I arrived on the shores of Croewick. It was there I saw another red-haired young woman standing in the doorway of her home with the full gleam of the houselight behind her. Through her green cotton dress patterned by small flowers, I could see the line of her body, the soft curve of her arms, legs and breasts. I was aware of one blemish that the dead girl had not possessed – a small brown mole on her right cheek. Otherwise, she was almost identical, her beauty mirroring the ghost of the one who had lain that day at my feet.

My hooves struck up sparks in the moonlight, scraping off stone. I heard myself, too, let slip a low whinny, one that mingled within the softness of the wind. It was this that drew her attention. She looked up from her place in the doorway. A few moments later and she was crossing the red sand and making her way in my direction, a squeal of laughter escaping her as she ran.

'It's a horse...' she said.

And then she stopped. It was as if she recognised me and knew I was not an ordinary steed. She took in my colouring – dirty brown, stained and soiled by the task I had taken on for myself over the last few years. She saw, too, the heaviness of my hooves with their iron shoes covered with the green scum of the sea, the pinkness of my muzzle cloaked with foam like the spume of waves.

'No...'

At that moment, a thought flashed through my head. I wondered if the dead girl might be her sister, that somehow a message of my true and ugly nature had been passed to her by that lost spirit. She seemed aware I had carried flesh similar to her own on my back, transporting those who were kin to her to the very darkness of death. No wonder she looked frightened and afraid. No wonder terror criss-crossed the paleness of her face.

Still, I decided to approach her, my muscles quivering as I circled where she stood, moving forward and backward as a real horse might do, while at the same time, trembling with excitement at the thought that she might be high upon my back a short time later, anticipating the prospect of her skin brushing against mine.

'Come on,' I willed her. 'Come on…'

She shook her head, ignoring my closeness, the way I brushed against her shoulder.

'Come on…'

'Wait!' she said and then she was running, the white calves of her legs flashing as she made her way in the direction of her home. I saw her step in the direction of an outhouse, its dim light shrouded by dirt smearing the window. A short time later and she was back at my side, carrying a cobwebbed black harness and bridle in her arms. She blew the dust off its surface, swishing it clean with the sleeve of her cotton dress. 'I'll ride on you if you wear this,' she muttered.

I shied away from her when she said this, fearful that this might mean a surrender to her will, allowing a human to take control of me for the first time since my parents had been alive.

'Come on,' she willed me. 'Come on.'

She was carrying some seaweed, brushing it against my neck back and forth, back and forth. It was as if she was trying to reassure me with the familiar tang of salt, a texture known to me from a thousand journeys through the surge of water, a rider perched high above me, grasping hold of my mane…

'Mas e 'chluasag dhut a' ghaineamh
Mas e leabaidh dhut an fheamainn
Mas e 'n t-iasg do choinnlean geala
Mas e na ròin do luchd-faire…'

'If it is thy pillow the sand
 If it is thy bed the seaweed
 If it is the fish thy candles bright
 If it is the seals thy watchmen…'

She sang it more sweetly than Calum Seonag had done the night of his death. In contrast to his sprawling incoherence, her voice possessed the clarity of water, rising and falling in a seamless cascade of notes. Each sound chilled and washed over me, making me tremble with tenderness for the red-haired girl who was by my side.

'Dh'òlainn deoch ge b' oil le càch e
 De dh'fhuil do chuim 's tu 'n déidh do bhàthadh…'

'I would drink, though all would detest it,
 of your heart's blood after your drowning…'

It was then I gave in to her, feeling the weight of the bridle on my back, the reins slipping over my head. And all the time she was singing the chorus of the song in a quiet hushed way, her hand soft on my neck as she caressed my mane with her fingers.

'Ò hì shiùbhlainn leat
 Hì ri bhò hò ru bhì
 Hì ri bhò hò rinn o ho
 Ailein Duinn, ò hì shiùbhlainn leat…'

'Ò hì, I would go with thee
 Hì ri bhò hò ru bhì
 Hì ri bhò hò rinn o ho
 Brown-haired Alan, ò hì, I would go with thee…'

The warmth of her breath blew in my ears when she clambered on my back. 'Ò hì shiùbhlainn leat,' she repeated once again. 'Whither thou goest, I will go with thee.'

And then I felt her fingers take control of me, steering my head in the direction she wished me to take. Secure in this woman's gentleness and love, it was a turn that I longed to follow, content that the full stretch of this beach marked the edge of my new pasture and I would never step into the ocean again. No more would I bear the dead upon my back, bring their bruised and broken corpses into shore.

I knew, too, that my new love held sway over me with a sweetness and tenderness I had never come across before. As the wind lapsed and the sea seemed to stop its rolling, I felt a change taking place within my heart and body. My hide was softening, becoming skin. My hooves were being transformed into feet. Even my teeth were shifting, reducing in size.

I was becoming human once again.

SOURCES AND INSPIRATIONS

I am grateful to all those who helped and inspired me in the creation of these pages. Clearly it would be impossible to acknowledge all the sources for the stories and poems they contain. However, the following are extremely important. I would like especially to thank the writer Lloyd Jones whose book, *Mr Pip*, sent me back to Charles Dickens' masterpiece, *Great Expectations*, encouraging me to read it in a new and exciting way. His work allowed me to combine its ideas with the rock song *Should I Stay Or Should I Go?* by the Clash and the work of the late Iain Crichton Smith – whose book *The Village* played an important part in the coming together of *Small Expectations*.

Various collections of folk-tales and Gaelic songs have also been crucial to its creation. These include the many stories that involve the uisge (or water horse, kelpie, nguggle) in all its various guises in the folklore of Northern Scotland. Other legends like the tale of the Cave Of Gold in Skye and Effie MacQueen's enforced exile from St Kilda form the basis of 'Scenes of Hebridean Haunting Part 2'. Gaelic love-songs appear elsewhere. My thanks go to both Maoilios Caimbeul and my fellow former-Nicolsonian and Gaelic singer Mairead Stiùbhart for her help in all of this.

Other books and stories also appear throughout the book. 'Voices In The Hebrides 3 – The Tongue' is visited by the ghost of the Russian writer Gogol and influenced by his short story, 'The Nose'. 'Scenes of Hebridean Haunting Part 1' was much influenced by the marvellous Northern Irish writer, David Park and his short story 'Crossing The River' which appeared recently in *Ox-Tales Water,* a collection published by Profile Books in 2009 to raise money for the charity Oxfam.

Both 'Dream–Glasses' and 'Porridge Galore' owe their genesis to other work. The former was inspired by a short story in Icelandic writer Gyrdir Eliason's fine collection *Stone Trees*

(Comma Press, 2008) and the latter by Compton Mackenzie's *Whisky Galore*. The beginnings of 'Unholy Mackerel' are to be found in a conversation I enjoyed with my friend and fellow-English teacher, Tom Clark. The children's story *The Tiger Who Came To Tea* by Judith Kerr also played an important role in the tale. Another evening that led to a poem was one I shared with Norman Macdonald, the BBC's man in Skye, who told me of Joe Strummer's connection with Raasay. My thanks go, too, to Iona Macdonald for her assistance in this.

A few of the poems – such as 'Ness Social Club' and 'Language' – previously appeared in *West-Coasters* (Cuan Ard Press, 2001) while 'Valentine's Day In The Hebrides' saw the light of day in the *New Shetlander*.

My thanks are also due to Yvonne Malcolmson, David Knowles, Sharon Blackie and Maggie Priest for the pleasure of their company in the weird and wonderful journey of creating *Small Expectations*.

A special note of gratitude has to go to Doug Robertson, an extraordinary artist who not only illustrated some of my 'guga' poems but also created the cover of this book. I owe him a great debt which I can never hope to repay.

Finally, one of the more difficult aspects of writing about the Western Isles is the limited number of both forenames and surnames to be found within its shores, forcing most writers to be over-careful in choosing names for their characters. In the story 'Valentine's Day In The Hebrides', I have tried to turn this into a virtue. I would like to apologise to any John Macleod (or his wife, companion or girlfriend) whose life is embroiled in confusion and suspicion because of the appearance of that name in that story. In my defence, the following should be noted.

It is not intended to be about you.

Donald S. Murray
September 2009

Two Ravens Press is the most northerly literary publisher in the UK, operating from a six-acre working croft on a sea-loch in the north-west Highlands of Scotland. Two Ravens Press is run by two writers with a passion for language and for books that are non-formulaic and that take risks. We publish cutting-edge and innovative contemporary fiction, non-fiction and poetry.

Visit our website for comprehensive information on all of our books and authors – and for much more:

- browse all Two Ravens Press books (print books and e-books) by category or by author, and purchase them online at a discount on retail price, post & packing-free (in the UK, and for a small fee overseas)

- there is a separate page for each book, including summaries, extracts and reviews, and author interviews, biographies and photographs

- read our regular blog about life as a small literary publisher in the middle of nowhere – or the centre of the universe, depending on your perspective – with a few anecdotes about life down on the croft thrown in. Includes regular and irregular columns by guest writers – Two Ravens Press authors and others

- sign up for our monthly e-newsletter, filled with information on our new releases and our authors, with special discounts, giveaways and other offers.

www.tworavenspress.com